WHEN LIFE WAS STILL

BOOKS BY JULIE A. RYAN

NOVELS

When Life Was Still
Book One: Ellen

When Life Was Still
Book Three: Amy

NOVELLAS

When Life Was Still
Book Two: Greta

POETRY

Relative Space

WHEN LIFE WAS STILL

Book Two: Greta

Julie A. Ryan

Printed in the United States of America

ISBN: 978-1-7331943-2-7 (paperback)
ISBN: 978-1-7331943-5-8 (e-book)

Book design and artwork by Haley Ryan
Illustrations by Julie A. Ryan

www.WhenLifeWasStill.com

This book is dedicated to my siblings, nephews, and nieces,
who have filled the corners of my heart with happiness.

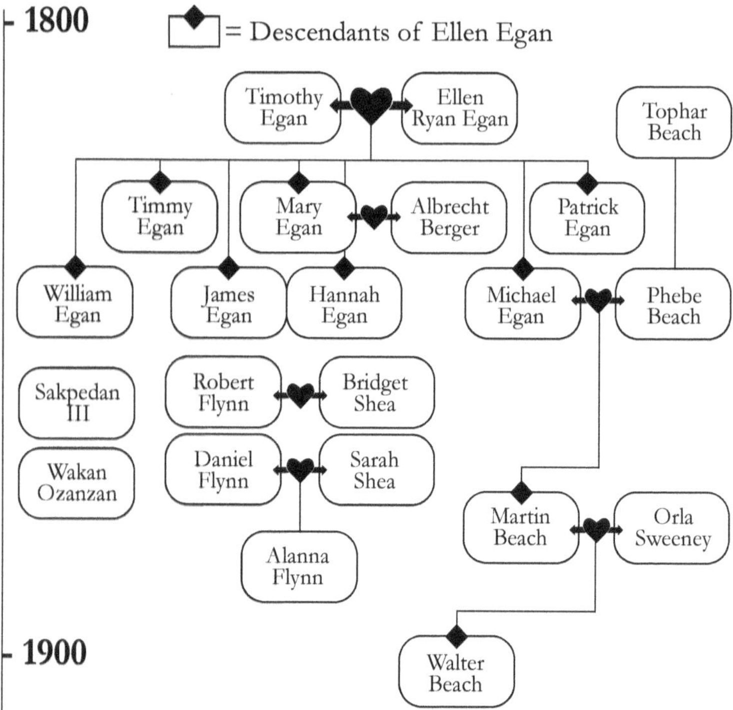

= Descendants of Ellen Egan
1800
Timothy Egan
Ellen Ryan Egan
Tophar Beach
Timmy Egan
Mary Egan
Albrecht Berger
Patrick Egan
William Egan
James Egan
Hannah Egan
Michael Egan
Phebe Beach
Sakpedan III
Robert Flynn
Bridget Shea
Wakan Ozanzan
Daniel Flynn
Sarah Shea
Martin Beach
Orla Sweeney
Alanna Flynn
1900
Walter Beach
2000

= Descendants of Anna Engel

Wilhelm Wagner
Frieda Kuhn
Johann Engel
Anna Buch Engel
Gottfried Hahn

Dieter Engel
Claudia Engel
Wendel Engel
Hermann Engel

Otto Wagner

Harold Engel
Elisabeth Engel
Paul Hahn

Orla Sweeney
Carl Wagner

Martha Wagner
Peter Eckmann

Janka Sawicki
Rojenia Kozlowski

John Redsun

Johnny Kozlowski

Joe Eckmann
Berta Hahn

Greta Eckmann

The Families of WHEN LIFE WAS STILL
Book One

= Intimate Relationship

Something Predictably Beautiful

from

WHEN LIFE WAS STILL

· BOOK ONE ·

"Choose a number greater than twenty."
"Add the digits of your chosen number."

WHEN LIFE WAS STILL

Book Two: Greta

DROSTE'S
CACAO
NET 125 g ℮

Dear Greta,

This is a place for your brilliant thoughts.

With Love,
Great-Grandmother
Anna Engel

This diary belongs to:

Greta Eckmann

March 19, 1924

Dear Gertie,

I'm sorry that we drifted apart. I will pray a Rosary novena for you every month until we meet again.

I thought for quite some time—an entire month as of today—about what words might be worth enough to put in this book of pages Great-Grandma Anna Engel has given to me. She told me to make note with my brilliant mind. I peered into my head and found I have nothing brilliant to say. So I decided to write what I would say to you if you were here.

With Love,
Greta

P.S. After I wrote my name in this diary, I noticed that Great-Grandma stitched the letter *E* on the pretty linen cover. The cover has a beautiful blue background that reminds me of you.

March 22, 1924

Dear Gertie,

You and I matched. We had the same strawberry-blonde hair, and I miss braiding yours. Do you remember how we said the exact same thing at the exact same time? Do you remember how we laughed at the same time? And cried at the same time? Do you remember when we last swam in the creek together? It was after we searched for cornflowers to pick. You always enjoyed anything blue. Do you enjoy floating where you are? How do you pass the time these days?

If words could build a bridge, I would use these pages to make my way to you so I could do whatever you're doing. Though I think you still know what I would say to you, I want to say it anyway.

With Love,
Greta

March 23, 1924

Dear Gertie,

You know that Great-Grandma Anna always gives me kerchiefs with edges she has crocheted as a gift. So I am happy about getting something different. Although she is quite old—ninety-nine years—I believe she still has her wits. When I undid the wrapping of this diary at my ninth birthday party, she smiled when she noticed my surprise.

Great-Grandma Anna made this diary over eight years ago. She is good at making books and made this for me when she saw what a special baby I was. She said I looked at the world around me and absorbed it. I'm not sure what *absorbed* means.

My party was in the church basement because Ma didn't feel up for knocking down the cobwebs in our house. Do you remember how we stuck our arms through her webs to make ourselves matching sleeves? How I miss giggling with you about stupid things.

The party was fun with all the cousins there. But it wasn't really a party without you.

With Love,
Greta

March 24, 1924

Dear Gertie,

I have to tell you about something. It happened when Great-Grandma Anna gave me these pages. She said my words have value. I smiled and said thank you because I'm polite. She put my hand in hers and held it for a long time.

I'm not sure I know what value is.

With Love,
Greta

March 31, 1924

Dear Gertie,

I'm sure you can see that I pen my words in English rather than our German tongue. *Vater* says it is important that I keep up with practicing my English and keep the Prussian parts of me only in my head.

If I have a Prussian head on a body born in America, am I still American? I will ask *Vater* tomorrow if he is in the mood for questions.

With Love,
Greta

April 1, 1924

Dear Gertie,

Today ~~*Vater*~~ Pa said if I can get to a point where I only think in English that would be good. He wants people to forgive us for having German Prussian ancestors and to know that we are Americans first.

With Love,
Greta

P.S. I'm afraid that I might forget and write freely in Low German. What if someone should someday steal my diary and pry into my thoughts? Do you think anyone could be awful enough to do that?

P.P.S. I'm learning that words can have so many meanings. I wish everyone spoke the language of mathematics. At school I'm learning that numbers are less dangerous than words. Mathematical problems have only one correct answer.

April 2, 1924

Dear Gertie,

Ma doesn't give a *scheisse* shit if I speak in German or English.
She spoke both when she was a girl. She doesn't give a shit about
anything other than the likker in her cup. Is that how you spell
likker in English? I think that is how it is written on our Kozlowski
moonshine jugs in the basement. All Ma has to say about the matter
is that *stein* is spelled the same in German and English, so she does
not have to choose which language is best. She says this to me in
German.

The length of the laugh that follows depends on how pickled
she is.

With Love,
Greta

April 3, 1924

Dear Gertie,

Today Pa said it is no issue to speak German among our family
and friends in Chance Hill. But he says I may not always live among
my kind. And I should prepare for that while my mind is still young.
I can't imagine why I should ever find myself in a place with people
who don't like me for my family's native tongue.

With Love,
Greta

April 7, 1924

Dear Gertie,

Today Miss Ingrid asked us students to write about a wish. I
didn't write anything because I don't know what a wish is.

With Love,
Greta

April 8, 1924

Dear Gertie,

It is because my young mind (Pa's word for it) enjoys learning that there are days I want to thank Ma for being so drunk the day she put me in school at the age of four. Other children in Chance Hill start at five or six. I don't know if she did it because I was extra smart or extra tall. Learning does come easier to me than some other children.

I never told you this. When I was four years old, I noticed that Pa was surprised when he returned from the Tavern and found I was a school girl. He must have still been tired from the War because he didn't fix the matter. He said to me, "You will keep up and make me proud." (Last week Miss Ingrid taught us about punctuating dialogue so we can be interesting writers.)

With Love,
Greta

April 9, 1924

Dear Gertie,

I like to make Pa proud. He is a quiet man, but he is a good man. That is what I've been hearing many people say lately. These days, when he is too tired, he talks with his eyes. I'm the only one in this house who understands his silent language. Tonight he looked at me and told me that he likes that I understand him. I told Pa with my eyes that it is easy to understand him. He smiled. I like it when Pa smiles, especially when it is in my direction.

With Love,
Greta

April 10, 1924

Dear Gertie,

I don't think I will ever thank Ma for my early start in school because words just drown around her. I wonder if it is my fault she is that way now. Do you blame me?

With Love,
Greta

April 11, 1924

Dear Gertie,

Tonight I asked Pa if he enjoyed helping America in the Great War because I know he likes helping people. Pa said that when he answered President Wilson's call to volunteer, he enjoyed being a telegraph operator in the beginning. But he didn't like it when a gun was put in his hands, and he was told to fight. Pa was sent to a place near where his grandparents were born in Prussia. When he was on the battlefield, he wished he was still working at the New Dresden Brewery. Pa didn't like the idea that he might be killing his German cousins when he fired his gun.

With Love,
Greta

April 17, 1924

Dear Gertie,

Can you see that I'm writing to you with my left hand?

It is five years now that I've been made to write with my right hand at school instead of my left hand. Remember how I complained to you about the pain? It still makes my hand hurt. I wonder why the way God made my hands is not all right at school.

With Love,
Greta

April 22, 1924

Dear Gertie,

I'm happy I have you to talk to because Ma isn't here much to share words with me. I have given up on having a dog to talk to. I stopped believing that she will bring home that dog she is always going to see a man about. Pa is always working at the Tavern and the little boys are not much for talking. The missing words in this house make me feel heavy. I wish I could hear what you're thinking right now. I hear your voice in my head a lot and wish I knew if it matched what you're thinking.

With Love,
Greta

April 23, 1924

Dear Gertie,

I should not have sat down to write. I just saw the time and have to go and do a fine job of milking the cows because Pa has the late shift at the Tavern. Did I ever tell you that for the longest time I thought *Tavern* was spelled *C-a-f-é?* This confused me when I was learning English, until Pa caught me staring at the sign. I was trying to make sense of it. He laughed and told me how *C-a-f-é* is pronounced. He said everyone still calls the business by its old name of the Tavern. I was five when the pretend sign was put up. Pa says the *Café* sign does a good job of keeping the liquor agents away.

After milking I have to get supper on for the boys. I don't mind making meals because I get to sing while I work. I wish Matt and Albert could be more useful. But they are only four-year-old babies. Only God knows where Ma will find herself tonight. I know it will not be in the kitchen. I have delayed myself by writing these words to you. But I am gladdened that I did. These words weigh less on paper than when they are inside my head.

With Love,
Greta

10

April 24, 1924

Dear Gertie,

Do you know what a flapper is?

Though I try not to get hit by Ma too often, I got punched in the face today. I told her this morning that I wanted to be the finest flapper in Chance Hill. She asked me if I knew what a flapper was. When I said yes, she hit me. I read in an old *Flapper* magazine in Great-Grandma Anna's store that flappers are not afraid to show their knees. I am not afraid of anything. But if I can't be a flapper, well, then I want a flapper with pretty knees to be my ma. My face hurts.

With Love,
Greta

P.S. I'm not sure I know what a flapper is. It must be something bad. I only told Ma I knew what a flapper was because I didn't want her to hit me for being stupid.

April 25, 1924

Dear Gertie,

Do you think there is goodness in everyone?

With Love,
Greta

April 26, 1924

Dear Gertie,

While I made supper, I heard a bluebird call your name.

When it said your name, it sounded happy. I hope that means you're happy where you are.

With Love,
Greta

May 1, 1924

Dear Gertie,

Great-Grandma Anna stopped by today to give me something
for my Name Day. As you know, there is no St. Greta and Ma didn't
want to choose a middle name for me when I was born. So St. Grata
is close enough. Grandma Anna told me she was waiting until I
was old enough to take care of her gift to me. It is the most beautiful
wooden box I have ever seen. It shines so much that it is warm. She
said Great-Grandpa Johann's brother Stephan made it. It has many
stars on it. I just finished counting and there 1,968 of them. It doesn't
seem possible that there can be that many on it, but he carved stars
within stars. I'm going to try counting the stars again after I recite
my prayers tonight. Sometimes I wish I could spend the rest of my
life counting.

Do you count the stars from where you are?

With Love,
Greta

P.S. In the star box is a book that Great-Grandma Anna's friend
Ellen Egan wrote. Do you know Ellen well? Some people called her
Frau Irish. Great-Grandma Anna and I called her Ellen. She carried
a heart-shaped rock in her pocket.

P.P.S. Great-Grandma Anna said she is giving this book and the
other things in the box to me, including the heart-shaped rock and
a photograph of me holding it. I have never seen a photo of me until
now. It is odd to look backward at time. Great-Grandma said Ellen
loved me during the first few years of my life and helped watch me
when there was no one else to care for me. She said that Ellen wrote
about me in her journal. Then she asked if I remembered her.

I do remember Ellen. My earliest memories are of her home.
Though I can't remember exactly how it looked, I know it smelled
like pine and had church benches to play on. There was also a large
box of toys that I played with when I visited her. Ellen's home was
always warm and it glowed, or maybe Ellen did.

12

When Ma is having one of her fits, I go to Ellen's home in my mind and hide under a church bench until the storm passes. When I have to go hide under the bench, I imagine Ellen is standing beside me, holding my hand in hers. I liked how her hands felt when she wrapped them around mine. When I was three years old, I remember thinking Ellen was trying to find something in my hands. And I hoped I would have something to give her someday.

May 2, 1924

Dear Gertie,

More Ellen memories have been knocking on my head. Here is another something I never told you, and you weren't there when it happened.

I remember being five years old and wanting Ellen to catch me if I jumped down from Great-Grandma Anna's largest maple tree. When I climbed to almost the top and looked down, I saw Ma standing on the ground bawling and screaming for me to come down. It made me feel good to see Ma cry about me. She put me up there because I was trying to escape a slap on my face. I figured Ma's fat thighs couldn't make it to the top, and I would be safe.

I knew that Ellen wouldn't be coming to help me because I saw her get put in a grave when I was almost four years old. But I still pictured her taking part in my life back when I was young.

When Great-Grandma Anna sent Ma inside the house and told me it was safe to come down the same way I went up—and said there would be no beating once I set foot on the ground—I climbed down. I knew I could believe everything Great-Grandma Anna said. I wish she could be my Ma.

With Love,
Greta

May 8, 1924

Dear Gertie,

William Egan gave the boys and me a ride home from the store today in his Tin Lizzie. He offered the ride to spare us the mile walk in the rain. He is really old, but William has always been kind to us.

The boys were asking all kinds of questions about his automobile and what each knob is for. They asked lots of questions about his "1914 Ford Model T," after William said that is what it is called. William was nice about it. He is nice in the same way Ellen was.

I remember when I was three and William's automobile was hitched to the wagon carrying Ellen's coffin. He drove her down the hill to her grave. I think of dirt every time I see William's Tin Lizzie. When I saw the dirt get tossed on Ellen's coffin, I remember thinking it was a shame that something so warm was getting put deep into the cold ground where nobody could cuddle up to it.

Life was colder after she was buried. But I still carry Ellen inside me. It is a spot that feels warm when I think about her. Though I don't think I believe in childish things like ghosts, sometimes I think Ellen is here with me.

With Love,
Greta

May 12, 1924

Dear Gertie,

Today I shared all my Ellen memories with Great-Grandma Anna in Low German because she spoke to me that way. I was afraid to do so at first, but Pa was not home. Once the words started tumbling down my tongue, I was so happy that I still remembered how to talk that way after going over a month of only speaking English. Great-Grandma told me many stories about the time she spent with Ellen in Wisconsin and Minnesota. Though they had a lot of fun together, it sounds as if life was really difficult when they

14

were young. I'm happy that times are so much easier now.

It was fun to have a lengthy conversation with someone who was born in Prussia and is the best at knowing how to speak the language—without any English drippings on it. I said these thoughts to Great-Grandma Anna and she reminded me that I come from Rhenish Prussians. She is proud of the Rhenish part because the Rhine River is where she was born.

Please don't tell Pa this. I refuse to stop thinking in German because it is my favorite language.

With Love,
Greta

June 1, 1924

Dear Gertie,

It is a wonder that Ellen knew how to treat people right. So many awful things happened to that woman. Many people around her died and disappeared. It is a good thing I've already had death come and touch me, otherwise I don't think someone my age should be reading about such things.

Ellen wrote about Great-Grandma Anna in her book. She was a good friend to Ellen. I wonder if I'll have a good friend someday who enjoys being with me. I haven't had a good friend since you left.

I'm looking forward to getting to the part in Ellen's book where she mentions me. I know I must be mentioned near the end part because Ellen was so old when she met me. I'm not the kind of person who cheats and reads the ending of a book before plowing through the rest, so I will wait patiently for me to appear.

With Love,
Greta

June 8, 1924

Dear Gertie,

I haven't been writing so often because, in the time I can spare, I have been reading Ellen's book, in case Great-Grandma Anna wants to talk about it in Low German.

I'm about halfway through, at the part where Ellen went to a hanging of two Dakota men at Fort Snelling with Grandpa Peter Eckmann when he was thirteen. When he was young, Grandpa Peter was thinking mean things about the Dakota and Ellen gave him a good dose of how to treat people right. It is nice to know something about Grandpa Peter. I was so young when he died that the only thing I can recall about him is what Pa told me he often said: "Judge no man by his appearance." Maybe that is because Grandpa Peter had a dent in the back of his head from a musket ball.

With Love,
Greta

June 9, 1924

Dear Gertie,

Even though Ellen's story is a mostly awful one so far, it makes me want to write about my life. Someday I want someone to see my own story in a book.

Great-Grandma Anna says that her Pa was a bookmaker. That is why she enjoys making books to give to people. I don't want to make books the way my grandparents did. But I do want to put my words on these blank pages I've been given. And I want to someday own books that I can share with other people in the way Great-Grandma Anna shares her books. Books seem to make people happy. At least, the books Great-Grandma Anna shares seem to change people.

With Love,
Greta

June 10, 1924

Dear Gertie,

I forgot to tell you I was promoted to Grade Six! And Miss Ingrid gave me her copy of *Main Street*. It is by Sinclair Lewis. I've been trying to read it today. I think I will have to set aside Ellen's book so that I can spend more time trying to understand *Main Street*, which is difficult reading for me. I haven't lived in a town with a street, so maybe that is why it is a difficult book for me. Maybe I'll understand it better when I'm older and have learned more. I feel bad for the boys who don't go beyond Grade Five because they are needed full-time on the farm at that age. They might never be able to understand *Main Street*.

Even though I am challenged, I'm happy that Miss Ingrid likes to share books with me. I want to read everything I can this summer. Great-Grandma Anna has quite a pile of reading for me at her store.

With Love,
Greta

July 6, 1924

Dear Gertie,

Today Great-Grandma Anna gave me a stack of blank paper and a charcoal pencil. She said Great-Aunt Claudia bought it in Minneapolis after visiting the Institute of Arts. She thought she might enjoy becoming an artist but was discouraged when her artwork looked nothing like Rembrandt's. I asked who Rembrandt was and Great-Grandma told me about his artwork.

She encouraged me to draw whatever I wanted to commit to the blank pages. Then she showed me some of her drawings. The birds she has drawn look real enough to fly off the page.

I wish Great-Grandma Anna could draw me and put wings on

17

me so I could fly away whenever I wanted to. If I had wings, I would fly to you.

> With Love,
> Greta

July 17, 1924

Dear Gertie,

I enjoy drawing. I don't know if I'm good at it; I may be poor at it like Great-Aunt Claudia. But I do know that I feel calm and in control of something when I try to capture on paper a picture that is in my head.

> With Love,
> Greta

August 17, 1924

Dear Gertie,

Time to write is hard to come by because Ma seems to be spending most of her time at the Tavern, and I have to do all the housework. But you know that I think of you daily and still pray a novena each month.

> With Love,
> Greta

September 29, 1924

Dear Gertie,

I just had the most terrifying thought while I was peeling potatoes. What if I'm responsible for my destiny instead of God? What if it is up to me to find my way to you?

> With Love,
> Greta

November 3, 1924

Dear Gertie,

Do you know that Dakota people are Americans now? President Coolidge says it has to be that way, no matter what someone's different opinion is. But people from China and Japan and other countries can't be Americans. I'm happy my people were allowed in the country before such rules were made. I'm afraid people with German backgrounds won't be let into America in the future because, according to Pa, some people still don't like them. Now that they're Americans, I wonder if the new rules will make Ma talk nicer about the Dakota people that pass through Chance Hill. I don't know why she is so mean to them. They never took anything of hers. Maybe she is jealous of how beautiful and wise they are. I wish Ma was a Dakota.

With Love,
Greta

November 5, 1924

Dear Gertie,

Miss Ingrid says we're fortunate to live in a country with free and fair elections. She voted for Robert La Follette for president of the United States. She said that any woman who didn't exercise her right to vote was wasting a vote for true democracy.

Ma didn't vote. She wasted a vote and wasted herself with Kozlowski's shine instead of thinking about things such as the next president.

What do you think keeps Ma from thinking about the future? Maybe she is too busy thinking about the past. Maybe it is my fault she is the way she is.

With Love,
Greta

November 6, 1924

Dear Gertie,

Miss Ingrid is disappointed that Calvin Coolidge won the election. But she said that even though she didn't vote for him, she will respect him as the president as long as he defends the Constitution and obeys the laws of human decency.

It is difficult to imagine a president who wouldn't uphold the Constitution or treat people decently. It is difficult for me to understand anyone who doesn't try to be decent to everyone. I don't understand Ma.

With Love,
Greta

November 16, 1924

Dear Gertie,

Happy Name Day to you! I made a cake for you today. And I spread strawberry jam on top in the shape of a *G* because I believe it is still your favorite topping.

I wish you could tell me if you still love strawberry jam.

With Love,
Greta

December 3, 1924

Dear Gertie,

I'm practicing for the Chance Hill School play. I have been given the most important part. Even though I'm only in Grade Six, I'm much better at reading and speaking English than any of the others in Seven or Eight where Miss Ingrid usually picks a narrator.

I have to narrate the play from memory. I would much rather read, of course. But Miss Ingrid says I have the best memory of anyone she knows. She says it is unusual to remember being a baby the way I do. If most people don't carry with them memories from their infancy, then what do they store in that space in their heads?

I'm happy to do what Miss Ingrid asks of me. She has always been kind enough. And I trust that she knows best how to do the Christmas play. I wish you could sit in the audience and watch me. I'm sure you would clap for me if you could.

With Love,
Greta

December 4, 1924

Dear Gertie,

Do you remember when I taught you how to clap in Morse code after Pa taught me? I wish every language was made of a pattern of dots and dashes. I wish people were made of dots and dashes so they would be easier to understand.

I miss talking to you in Morse code. After I put my pen down tonight, I'm going to clap "I love you." I hope you get the message.

· ·   · – · · – – – · · · – ·   – · – – – – – · · – ,

Greta

December 20, 1924

Dear Gertie,

The play is done. I think I did well. Pa and Miss Ingrid said I did. Ma didn't show up. Neither did the two men who were supposed to play piano and violin between my words. Without them there, I hummed the between music that they were supposed to play to distract the audience from the actors getting ready to come on stage for their scenes. I think it worked. The people in the audience smiled at me. And Miss Ingrid said I was brilliant to remedy the matter in that way.

Saint Nikolaus did remember to show up after the play this year. He wasn't pickled because he was played by William Egan instead of that drunk who usually does it. He was a good choice because he is as nice as I ever imagined Saint Nikolaus to be. What do you suppose it is that makes some people nice and some people awful?

With Love,
Greta

P.S. It felt good to have a voice that people heard.

December 22, 1924

Dear Gertie,

I just finished decorating the tree Pa brought in. I wish you could have helped me hang the tinsel.

With Love,
Greta

December 25, 1924

Dear Gertie,

We had Christmas dinner at noon this year because Ma went directly home after Mass, and Pa was home on time from visiting at the Tavern after Mass. He brought home *leberwurst* that he won in a drawing. We also had chicken, mashed potatoes, canned beans, and sauerkraut from the crock in the basement that Albert left his stocking in. I didn't tell Ma about the stocking because I didn't want him to get smacked on Christmas Day. I just fished it out and scooped the kraut into the pan. I have no idea why Albert put his stocking in there. But I do know it was difficult for me to swallow the kraut at dinnertime.

With Love,
Greta

December 27, 1924

Dear Gertie,

Heilige Johannes Tag! I wish you could have celebrated St.
John's Day with me this year. I noticed Great-Grandma Anna was
enjoying it. She smiled during the chanting of the three priests and
the singing of the four-part choir. After the High Mass, she did a
bit of reminiscing at her house party about Great-Grandpa Johann.
Though I never met him, he sounds as if he was a decent man. I
guess he was an important man, too, because he helped make the
church and the Tavern.

I wish I was old enough to sit at the card-playing table instead of
having to stay out of sight and watch after the children rolling in the
pile of coats on the bed. I enjoy playing euchre because I like seeing
the numbers on the cards dance around the table and in my head.

I enjoy keeping track of the patterns when I play card games
with Great-Grandma Anna. As it is with drawing, following
number patterns is another thing that makes me feel that I'm in
control. I enjoy being able to know what will probably happen next.
Great-Grandma Anna told me that I'm better at making predictions
than anyone she has known. But I can't imagine that it is a skill that
is useful in the way cooking and cleaning are.

With Love,
Greta

January 6, 1925

Dear Gertie,

It is 1925! I'm hoping for a good new year.

It was a nice Epiphany Mass this morning with the sun shining
through the ancestors' stained-glass windows. I wondered if Great-
Grandpa and Great-Grandma Engel were able to enjoy the sun
shining through their windows on previous Epiphany mornings. At
the same moment that I had that thought, I looked over at Great-
Grandma Anna and saw that she was acknowledging the beam

of sunlight pouring through her window. Or maybe the light was pouring out of Great-Grandma. I'm not sure where the light was coming from. I do know that Great-Grandma Anna is connected to the sun.

Do you think I'm odd for writing such things?

With Love,
Greta

January 18, 1925

Dear Gertie,

I truly enjoy mathematics. Numbers don't lie the way some religious words do. I don't know if I dare tell about my love of math to anyone but you. I think Miss Ingrid knows because she has been giving me advanced math books she borrowed from New Dresden High School.

On Friday she told me about Albert Einstein, who is an expert in physics. In case you don't know, physics is for studying the natural world and what makes it so. Albert Einstein was born in Germany and thinks about things in the world that haven't been thought about before. I wonder if he thinks of those things while he sits in church, in the way I do.

Don't you think it is wonderful that there are new thoughts to be had?

With Love,
Greta

January 19, 1925

Dear Gertie,

Do you think it is fine to spend time doing nothing but thinking? I like thinking about Einstein's Theory of Relativity that Miss Ingrid told me about. It helps me understand why I never feel I am at rest—other than that Ma and the boys are useless and do nothing to help around here. After considering his ideas about space and time, I found myself wanting to tell Mr. Einstein about my thoughts.

I want to travel faster than the speed of light so I can go back in time to when you were a part of my life. I often think about the best way to get from me to you. Should I find a way to be with you, or should I simply pray that it happens? Is God so powerful that He can cause me to have a desire too challenging for Him to fulfill?

With Love,
Greta

January 20, 1925

Dear Gertie,

Albert Einstein probably thinks about physics while sitting in a synagogue instead of a church because Miss Ingrid told me that he is Jewish. I've never met a Jewish person. I hope I get to know one someday.

Have you met any Jewish people where you are?

With Love,
Greta

February 8, 1925

Dear Gertie,

When I was sitting in church today, I wondered if religious truth is a real thing. Miss Ingrid told me to believe nothing unless it agrees with my own reason. This morning, I looked around at the heads in the pews in front of me and wondered what thoughts they held about religious truth.

Do you think it is all right for me to think when I'm in church?

With Love,
Greta

February 9, 1925

Dear Gertie,

Great-Grandma Anna has noticed my interest in mathematics. She is so old—one hundred years at the end of this month—yet so perceptive! When I was visiting her at the store today, she told me that I can keep the store records for her as long as she is alive.

After she told me that, she reached up to a shelf and pulled down her copy of *Principia Mathematica* by Isaac Newton that has been sitting on her store shelf ever since I can remember. She blew the dust off and handed it to me. Great-Grandma said she has been waiting for someone to read the whole thing ever since it came into her possession back in Wisconsin. She said because I'm so brilliant, I would probably enjoy the contents of the book more than anyone she knows.

The *Principia* is even older than Great-Grandma; it was published in 1729. I'm worried that the pages will crumble. But I'm going to start carefully reading it as soon as I have a spare moment.

With Love,
Greta

February 10, 1925

Dear Gertie,

I might never sleep again. When I opened the *Principia* to start reading it, I heard a scream that sounded as if it was from another world. Then I saw old bloody fingerprints on the pages and tossed the book under my bed.

Now I'm afraid to sleep with that book under my bed. But I'm also afraid to crawl under my bed and retrieve it.

With Love,
Greta

Greta

February 11, 1925

Dear Gertie,

Do you think I'm childish for sleeping with Ellen's heart-shaped rock? It makes me feel safe even though that bloody book is still under my bed.

With Love,
Greta

February 15, 1925

Dear Gertie,

Why do you suppose men don't have to wear head coverings in church? I've been noticing there are differences in how men and women are expected to behave in different settings.

With Love,
Greta

February 16, 1925

Dear Gertie,

Great-Grandma Anna gave me my birthday present early because I complained to her that Ma won't think about getting light bulbs in our house. I've burnt all the candles we had. And the kerosene lamp is kept in Ma and Pa's room that I'm not allowed to go in.

I was at Great-Grandma's store when I complained to her. She told me to turn around and shut my eyes. While I stood there with my eyes closed, I heard paper rustling. Great-Grandma stepped in front of me and told me to open my eyes. She put the package in my hands and said it was for my birthday. Great-Grandma gave me a flashlight.

I'm looking forward to being able to shine the light on my diary and write to you after the boys go to sleep. I wish I could leave my

27

flashlight on all night long because I'm more afraid of the bloody book under my bed when it is dark in my room than when it is lit up. Great-Grandma said I can come to her when I need a new battery. But I plan to use my light sparingly so that it doesn't burn out too quickly.

With Love,
Greta

February 19, 1925

Dear Gertie,

Today was my birthday. But it was not acknowledged by anyone because we are busy preparing for Great-Grandma Anna's wake. It will be in the parlor of her house. I hope the day is warm because the house can't possibly hold all who loved her, and we will have to take turns standing outside when we pay our respects.

The sound of St. John Church's *tode glocke* sounded different when it tolled for her—more hollow.

With Love,
Greta

February 24, 1925

Dear Gertie,

Ma managed to anger her cousins and aunts and uncles after the funeral. She claimed that, as the youngest granddaughter, she has a right to Grandma Anna's house and valuables. Pa had to haul her outside while she was screaming that Grandma Anna would want her to have it all. He had to sit on her until she calmed down. She is an embarrassment to me. She was drunk. But there is no excuse for anyone to act as stupidly as she does. My embarrassment was replaced by honor as I realized that Great-Grandma Anna had thought before she died to make me the owner of her most valuable possession—Ellen's wooden star box of keepsakes. It is mine and nobody can fight me for it. I'm going to move it to a better hiding place to make sure Ma doesn't get her hands on it. Things like that are too valuable for a person like her to have. She wouldn't know what to do with meaningful items.

Actually, I guess I don't know what to do with all the things Great-Grandma Anna has given to me, other than hold on to them and keep them safe.

With Love,
Greta

March 1, 1925

Dear Gertie,

Now that Great-Grandma Anna is dead, I feel guilty for not finishing reading Ellen's book. I only got halfway through—to the Dakota hanging part—before I abandoned it for other reading. I have enough bad things in my own life that I don't want to read the rest of Ellen's book right now. I will never be able to discuss Ellen's writing with Great-Grandma Anna. I won't be able to discuss anything with her again. Death is so final.

With Love,
Greta

March 7, 1925

Dear Gertie,

My arm is still sore where Father Richter grabbed it. He pulled me out of the confessional and told me to never again confess that I believe in mathematics more than God. I might never get done with the penance he gave me.

What do you think would happen if I confess to Father Richter how I feel about him? Sometimes I wish I could be the kind of person who dares to find out such things. I want to be the kind of person who dares not follow the straight line set before me in Father Richter's sermons. I wonder if Father Richter has ever ventured beyond the boundaries of the Ten Commandments. If he does, and confesses those sins to a priest, do you think he gets his arm squeezed?

With Love,
Greta

March 8, 1925

Dear Gertie,

Do you think some people prefer not to think for themselves? Is it possible that life is easier to live that way? Maybe I've been going about life the wrong way.

With Love,
Greta

March 9, 1925

Dear Gertie,

Do you think pain is necessary?

With Love,
Greta

March 15, 1925

Dear Gertie,

What do you think the people of St. John's Church would be doing if the Ten Commandments didn't keep them penned in?

With Love,
Greta

May 17, 1925

Dear Gertie,

Do you think behavior is more important than beliefs? I seem to understand the actions of people better than their words.

With love,
Greta

July 4, 1925

Dear Gertie,

I seem to understand trees and clouds better than people. It is when I'm outside that I feel my head is calm, and I can breathe. I'm tempted to carve a face in the bark of the maple tree you and I used to climb and call it my friend.

With Love,
Greta

September 18, 1925

Dear Gertie,

Today Miss Ingrid told us about her summer trip to Europe. I asked her if she saw any Rembrandts while she was there. She said she did see his work in museums. She said she also enjoyed seeing an opera called *The Ring*. It was composed by a man named Richard Wagner. She said his works always remind her that art makes life worthwhile.

I like art too. I still have some of that drawing paper Great-Grandma Anna gave me. I think I'll pull out my charcoal pencil and draw my life into something worthwhile. I'll see if Matt and Albert would like to draw with me. They deserve a meaningful life too.

Is your life meaningful?

With Love,
Greta

September 21, 1925

Dear Gertie,

Miss Ingrid brought her phonograph to school today. She played "I've Got the Yes! We Have No Bananas Blues" and Bessie Smith's "Downhearted Blues."

She asked us to write our own lyrics for a blues song. I've never written one before. A blues song is similar to a poem, which I've also never written before. I'm happy that we will work on this assignment all week because this is something I'm not very good at doing.

This is what I have for my song so far:

> *Sorrowful sorrow*
> *Will hand me my tomorrow*
> *And every day after that.*
>
> *It'll come banging on my front door*
> *And I won't think*
> *To send it back*
>
> *'Cause sorrowful sorrow*
> *Can be knocked down with moonshine*
> *As I dance across the floor.*
>
> *But sorrowful sorrow*
> *Will always get up in the morning,*
> *And bring me something more.*

With Love,
Greta

September 22, 1925

Dear Gertie,

Do you think I'll ever own a phonograph?

With Love,
Greta

September 30, 1925

Dear Gertie,

Miss Ingrid said that 40,000 Ku Klux Klansmen marched on Washington D.C. this month. She showed us pictures in her newspaper. They are marching for Christianity and they hate Catholics. I don't understand why. I only know Catholics and have nobody to ask what is so dreadful about Catholics. We Catholics *are* Christians. And some of us are good people.

I also don't understand how, after going through the Civil War, there can still be 40,000 people left in this country who also hate people who aren't white. I don't understand why people should be hated just because of their appearance.

Hating people for the color of their skin and hair makes no more sense than having people hate me because I'm Catholic, or because of the ragged clothes I'm forced to wear because my ma doesn't bother to sew when my dresses get torn. Though I've started sewing patches on, I'm not very good at it. If I have any spare time, I'm going to practice my stitching so my repair efforts look more respectable.

I saw in the newspaper pictures that the Ku Klux Klan wears hats that are white and tiny and pointed at the top. I wonder if the men who wear those hats have tiny pointed heads.

With Love,
Greta

November 16, 1925

Dear Gertie,

Miss Ingrid was talking about President James Madison today. She gave each of us a piece of paper that had one of his thoughts on it. This is the thought I was given:

A popular Government, without popular
information, or the means of acquiring it,

is but a Prologue to a Farce or a Tragedy;
or, perhaps both. Knowledge will forever
govern ignorance: And a people who
mean to be their own Governors, must
arm themselves with the power which
knowledge gives.

Miss Ingrid went around the room, asking what we thought the words on our paper meant. I said I thought my words meant that paying attention in school is important so that students can learn as much as possible. Miss Ingrid nodded and asked why it is important to learn as much as possible. I said so that we can be the rulers instead of those who are ruled. I then said that if one of us happens to become president of the United States, we should make sure that we are as smart as we can possibly be so that other countries with bad intent don't find a way to rule over us. Miss Ingrid smiled and said she thought I was correct. She added that it would be horrifying to have a president who could be easily influenced by malevolent foreign powers.

Then Ernie Shepley blurted out, "Why is Greta concerning herself with becoming smart? Girls can't become president of the United States."

Miss Ingrid bit down on her bottom lip and took a deep breath before she responded, "You are correct that girls cannot become president. But women who are at least thirty-five years of age can become president."

All the boys in the room gasped. Then Ernie shouted, "She's pulling our legs, fellas. Women can't be president of the United States." The boys erupted with laughter as the girls looked at one another in silence.

The boys' laughter was interrupted by Miss Ingrid. She said, "You're wrong, Ernie. I am not joking. Someday there will be a woman in charge of this country." Silence swallowed the boys' laughter as us girls looked at one another and smiled.

With Love,
Greta

Greta

November 20, 1925

Dear Gertie,

If a woman became president, what do you think this country would be similar to? If a woman became president, do you think women would be allowed to do everything that men do and go everywhere they go? I think I would prefer not to be in the kitchen for the rest of my life.

With Love,
Greta

January 4, 1926

Dear Gertie,

Do you know of anyone who is all good or all bad? I'm having difficulty seeing any good in Ma. She pulled me out of bed when she got home last night and gave me a beating. When I asked her what I did wrong, she said I was born.

With Love,
Greta

January 22, 1926

Dear Gertie,

Do you think I'm horrid for planning to hit Ma with the heart-shaped rock that I sleep with the next time she hauls me out of bed?

Last night I had a dream that Ma hit me on the head one too many times and I died. Part of me is fine with dying and causes me to think I should just let her hit me. The other part of me thinks I should defend my right to live a decent life.

Do you think life can be decent?

With Love,
Greta

35

March 7, 1926

Dear Gertie,

I would like to have anyone other than Father Richter teach me about human nature and life. He thinks women are wayward and need men to rule over them.

With Love,
Greta

March 14, 1926

Dear Gertie,

If every person was forced to listen to the sermon of a scientist on Sundays instead of a priest, what do you think this country would be like?

With Love,
Greta

March 21, 1926

Dear Gertie,

Do you think God somehow profits from the existence of evil?

With Love,
Greta

April 18, 1926

Dear Gertie,

Do you think there is a place without priests?

With Love,
Greta

June 13, 1926

Dear Gertie,

This summer I'm reading a book from Miss Ingrid called *The Great Gatsby* by a man called F. Scott Fitzgerald. Miss Ingrid said she has a library in her parents' house that is getting too full. So she is giving some of her books away.

F. Scott Fitzgerald is a friend of a friend of Miss Ingrid. Mr. Fitzgerald (I will call him that because I don't know if he prefers to be called F. Scott, Scott, or maybe F.) gave the book to Miss Ingrid at a party they were both attending in St. Paul. She offered to pay him for it. But he said the book is a flop and is giving it away to anyone who will take it.

Miss Ingrid has family in St. Paul on a street called Summit Avenue. She goes there a lot on the weekends. Ma gripes about Miss Ingrid being too good to spend time at the Tavern on the weekends. I think Ma is just jealous that *she* isn't good enough to spend time on Summit Avenue. I wonder if Summit Avenue is like East Egg—a place where Gatsby lives. It would be a real dream if I could go to a place like East Egg or Summit Avenue. Miss Ingrid makes it sound spectacular. She said the electric lights are left on all night long. Even at night people stroll on the sidewalks by the streets because, I suppose, they have leisure time. She takes electric streetcars to get to the interesting places in the city when she doesn't want to drive.

Do you think I'll get to go anywhere interesting enough to write about before I see you again?

With Love,
Greta

July 5, 1926

Dear Gertie,

Yesterday Pa took the boys and me to Memorial Park in New Dresden to celebrate the 150th anniversary of the Declaration of Independence. From a food cart, Pa bought a scoop of ice cream that sat on top of a banana for us to share; it was delicious! A banana is a delightfully odd food. I hope to have another one sometime. Later in the day, Pa bought an ice cream cone for the four of us to share. The boys fought over who would get to eat the last piece of the cone. So Pa crushed it in his hand into four equal pieces. We each had the last piece of the cone. It was grand to have two interesting treats in one day.

Ma wasn't with us, so Pa said we could stay until we were ready to go home. Pa was in quite a great mood. He even danced the polka with me in front of the band shell where the Novak Brothers band was playing. Matt and Albert laughed at us as we danced.

We saw a captured German Howitzer. And Pa laughed when I asked if Germany might want it back now that our fighting with them is done. When I asked him why he was laughing, he said, "Some fights are never done. It is good to hang on to artillery." I don't like the idea of hanging on to weapons. It seems as if people who possess weapons want to fight someone. But I suppose Pa is more wise than I am about such matters.

None of us had any desire to return home (including Pa). So we stayed at Memorial Park until after we saw fireworks exploding in the sky. To experience a banana and color exploding in the black sky on the same day makes me believe that life could be enjoyable.

As we sat and watched everyone pack up their belongings and leave the park, Pa pointed up at the crescent moon and said, "A rabbit lives up there."

The boys dropped their mouths open and stared at the moon.

When I didn't react, Pa said, "You don't believe me, Greta?"

I didn't want to upset Pa on our perfect day by being truthful. But then I saw him smile, so I said, "I don't think there is a rabbit that can jump that high."

Pa laughed hard, then pointed at the moon again. "Remind me in twenty days, and I'll show you the rabbit on the moon."

Everyone else had left the park, so Pa stood up and held his hand out to me. I took his hand and stood up even though I didn't want to leave that perfect day behind. Pa looked into my eyes. I could see that he didn't want to leave it either.

With Love,
Greta

July 19, 1926

Dear Gertie,

I just finished reading *The Great Gatsby*. I've been thinking about bootlegging. I don't understand why selling liquor isn't made easier so people don't have to sneak around and get bad reputations. In Chance Hill everybody drinks liquor and buys it wherever they can. And they carry it in a boot if their pockets are full.

What is it like to be in a place without liquor?

With Love,
Greta

July 24, 1926

Dear Gertie,

Pa took us outside tonight when it got dark. He pointed up at the moon. "Can you find it?" he asked. The boys and I looked for a long time but didn't see it. Pa said, "If you believe in something enough, you can make it appear."

Right after Pa said that, I saw the rabbit!

Do you see the rabbit on the moon from where you are?

With Love,
Greta

August 10, 1926

Dear Gertie,

A woman named Gertrude swam across the English Channel. Since you have the same name, wouldn't it be nice if you also knew how to swim as well as her?

With Love,
Greta

September 29, 1926

Dear Gertie,

When we were studying geography, Miss Ingrid talked about the Soviet Union. She said the leaders there like to call someone "enemy of the people" if they disagree with the Soviet Union. And they hurt them in lots of way too. Why would someone run a country that way?

I'm glad I live in America where people are better at matters of right and wrong, and leaders know how to act properly. I feel lucky to be born in a democracy where Congress would put a president in his place if he started acting like an autocrat or dictator. I used to think that every country was like America. But I'm learning a lot about different kinds of governments from Miss Ingrid.

With Love,
Greta

November 3, 1926

Dear Gertie,

Sometimes I forget to say all my bedtime prayers. After I pray the novena for you, I often fall asleep thinking about Einstein's cosmological constant and spacetime. My mind drifts to a place that is dark. Then, before I know it, it is morning.

Do you think God forgives me?

With Love,
Greta

December 13, 1926

Dear Gertie,

E pluribus unum—that is Latin for "out of many, one." Miss Ingrid says that is a very important thing to remember about our country when we disagree with our fellow countrymen about something. She said that viewing ourselves as part of one shared space helps inspire Americans to work together and consider everyone's beliefs.

Though I'll never confess this to Father Richter, I think *e pluribus unum* is a more meaningful message than the entire Latin Mass.

With Love,
Greta

February 9, 1927

Dear Gertie,

I just realized today that what I thought was a letter E on my diary is actually the Greek letter *sigma*. It is also called a "summation" symbol.

I made that discovery when Miss Ingrid borrowed an algebra text book for me from New Dresden's high school. I flipped to the middle of the book and saw the symbol and asked Miss Ingrid what the letter E represented. She told me what it was and said that a formula may require the addition of many variables. So sigma notation allows us to write a long sum in a concise way. I believe that I will enjoy sigma notation because I like saving time.

I regret that Great-Grandma Anna is no longer here to ask her why she put that on the diary she made for me. Do you suppose she knew I would enjoy mathematics and being concise?

It seems that adults may know things about the future that children don't. Pa is like that in some ways. He seems to know many things I don't. But he also seems too weary to take the time to know me the way Great-Grandma Anna did.

I don't think Ma knows anything. Nothing meaningful comes to mind when I sift through all the memories I have of her.

With Love,
Greta

March 22, 1927

Dear Gertie,

Pa died last night. Nothing is constant.

With Love,
Greta

P.S. I'm having a lot of trouble breathing right now. I think Pa took the air in my lungs with him when he departed. If you happen to come across my air, please send it back my way.

March 23, 1927

Dear Gertie,

I think I'm a different person than I was when Pa was here.

With Love,
Greta

March 26, 1927

Dear Gertie,

Grandma Martha was sobbing at Pa's funeral. My Eckmann aunts and cousins did a good job of comforting her.

I wish I could have comforted her. But Grandma Martha's brother Otto was always around her at the funeral. I've only seen him a few times. But I've seen him enough to know that he frightens me. There is something in his eyes that I find unsettling.

With Love,
Greta

Greta

March 28, 1927

Dear Gertie,

I wonder if I sit in other people's memories the way they sit in mine.

With Love,
Greta

March 29, 1927

Dear Gertie,

Do you think I'm in a black hole? Do you think black holes exist?

Do you think I exist?

With Love,
Greta

March 31, 1927

Dear Gertie,

I looked for the moon tonight but couldn't find it.

With Love,
Greta

April 1, 1927

Dear Gertie,

I'm trying to move past matters of death and get back into the routine of life.

How do you think Pa is doing? I miss him. Though he never talked much after getting back from the War, he brought calm to this place. Without him around, Ma makes everything upside-down. And even without talking, she makes everything noisy.

43

I heard someone say at his funeral that Pa stepped in front of the Model T on purpose, to be free of Ma. Then the man laughed.

Do you think it is Ma's fault? Do you think Pa tried to get run over? If he did, I'm sorry that the boys and I weren't enough for him to stay on Earth.

Do you think I can count on anyone to stay in my life?

With Love,
Greta

April 6, 1927

Dear Gertie,

My arms are so heavy. I don't know how I'll get the potatoes peeled tonight.

My feet are heavy too. The days are simply too long for me to pick up my feet and step through them.

I want to dive into the potato pot and close the lid. If I do, how long do you think it will be until someone comes looking for me? Do you think there is a better place for me than the potato pot?

With Love,
Greta

April 8, 1927

Dear Gertie,

Do you remember when I told you that, instead of crying, you should whisper your desire for better days to the stars? I wish you were here to tell me that now.

With Love,
Greta

April 9, 1927

Dear Gertie,

Tonight I told Ma we were out of flour. She told me to shut up and be content with what I have. That is the first thing she has said to me since Pa died. She has been gone most of the nights, which is fine with me.

Though the boys and I are doing fine without Ma, Grandma Martha has been stopping by to check on us a lot since the funeral. She makes the drive out from Freedale more often, now that she knows Ma is around less often. I don't think she ever liked Ma.

Grandma Martha is really sad. I feel bad about her losing her son, especially if he walked in front of the automobile on purpose. I think Pa was her favorite child.

Do you think I deserve flour?

With Love,
Greta

April 10, 1927

Dear Gertie,

After Ma got home tonight, she hauled me out of bed. When she threw the first punch, I held up the heart-shaped rock in front of my face. Ma whacked her knuckles into it. She howled like a wounded dog and ran out of the room.

I think that will be the last time she hits me.

With Love,
Greta

April 11, 1927

Dear Gertie,

Miss Ingrid said that Martin and Orla Beach of St. Owen are looking for someone to be a chore boy and help do the bookkeeping

45

for Sweeney's General Store. She said because they are elderly, they are looking for a boy with an eighth-grade education to help them. They believe that boys are best at mathematics. Miss Ingrid said to them that I was by far better with numbers than any of the boys she has ever known and that I have a superior intellect compared to all my classmates. Mr. and Mrs. Beach want the person who helps them to move in with them. They can't find anyone good enough in St. Owen or Rottenburg and are now considering students in Chance Hill. I don't know why it should be such a challenge to find someone to help out.

I was told that completing an interview with Mrs. Beach is a requirement. Perhaps she has high standards. Miss Ingrid said if I took the position and moved in with Mr. and Mrs. Beach, she would insist that they also provide me with the opportunity to go to high school. Miss Ingrid doesn't want to see a brain like mine not get used.

Do you think I'll actually go to a high school? If I get to go to a high school, I will make a point of reading every book in the library.

I'm going to try my best to get the job with Mr. and Mrs. Beach so I can go to high school.

With Love,
Greta

April 22, 1927

Dear Gertie,

Mrs. Beach came to the schoolhouse to meet me. She said that she was impressed by my careful diction. She said I don't seem the least bit German and could fit with the Irish folks of St. Owen with my reddish coloring. I think she liked my polite nature because she smiled when I called her Mrs. Beach and said I should call her Orla.

William Egan put in a good word for me because Martin Beach is his brother's son. Though I'm not bold enough to ask, I do wonder why William and Martin don't have the same last name.

Martin and Orla want to hire someone who is good with numbers to help them find a way to hang on to more of their money. All it took was one look at Orla and her fine taste in clothing and accessories for me to realize it wouldn't take any math to find the solution to their money trouble. She simply needs to stop spending so much of it.

Orla said she will get back to me with her decision. I'm afraid I won't get the job because my best dress that I wore to the meeting looked like a dishrag next to Orla's attire. I think trivial matters, such as clothing, are important to her.

I hope my trivial ability to blend in with the folks in St. Owen because of my strawberry-blonde hair matters enough to cause Orla to choose me as her chore boy.

With Love,
Greta

May 22, 1927

Dear Gertie,

Charles Lindbergh flew from New York to Paris. I wonder if I'll get to fly anytime soon. I relish the idea of not being stuck to the same ground I've always been on.

Do you like flying?

With Love,
Greta

June 2, 1927

Dear Gertie,

Ma is letting me leave to live in St. Owen!!

After Miss Ingrid told me that Orla and Martin chose me to be their chore boy, I waited until Ma was in a decent enough mood to ask her if I may leave. She said she will ship Matt and Albert off to live with Grandma Martha, and the aunts and cousins, in Freedale because she doesn't have time to keep an eye on them.

I hope the boys don't have to listen to too much crying in Freedale. Grandma is still sad about Pa dying. And both aunts are still sad about losing their husbands in the War nine years ago. But they will have fun with our cousins and the boys will probably get to go to high school in Freedale when they're old enough. So my leaving home has turned into a good situation for them.

I have to go to the Tavern to telephone Orla and tell her the good news. I hope I didn't wait too long for Ma to be in a good mood and that Orla is still interested in hiring me.

With Love,
Greta

June 22, 1927

Dear Gertie,

I moved in with Orla and Martin two weeks ago. I live with them above Sweeney's General Store. They have a phonograph! Orla's grandfather built the store, and it has been run by the family ever since. I've been too busy straightening out the bookwork to explore much of St. Owen; however, I was out on St. Owen Lake. I went with Orla and Martin after church last Sunday when they forced me to take a break from my duties. There are lots of cattails at the lake's edge.

Do you remember the day we held cattails under our noses and pretended we were men in search of adventure? I remember it. I seem to remember everything—good and bad. I would like to know how to let go of the weight of bad memories so that it is easier to flit through life as Orla does. Should I ask Orla how to flit? Maybe one simply needs to obtain a chore boy so she can focus on flitting. I'm simply not the flitting type. If I had a chore boy, I would probably help him do his job so that he would have spare time to read books and go to high school. I think you would giggle with me about the word *flit* if you were here.

With Love,
Greta

June 30, 1927

Dear Gertie,

I miss Matt and Albert almost as much as I miss you. I hope they are doing well. They are probably enjoying living in Freedale. According to what I've read about town life, I think it suits them. I still wonder what it is like to live in a town and to be close to people. How is there enough air for everyone to breathe in a town?

I won't be starting high school this fall. Orla says that I deserve a break from schooling since I'm so far ahead for my age. She said I should take time to experience the good life while I'm young. She promised that she will get me enrolled in high school next year. She says in the meantime she will purchase any books that I would like to study while I keep the record books and run the store.

I want an entire library of books. But it is difficult to imagine having time to study school books while doing this job. So I asked Orla if she would please purchase Wagner's *The Valkyrie* for playing on the phonograph and subscribe to the *St. Paul Pioneer* newspaper. I would like to listen to art and keep up with current events. Orla reacted as if she didn't actually expect me to request anything of her.

With Love,
Greta

P.S. Am I horrid for thinking that Orla is keeping me from high school for selfish reasons? The nine-mile drive to and from Gaston each day would be quite a commitment for her and Martin. Am I selfish for wishing I was a Gaston town girl instead of a St. Owen chore boy?

July 2, 1927

Dear Gertie,

I like running Sweeney's Store when I'm alone and the only one in charge. Being in charge suits me. When I'm at the store and no one stops by, I sometimes turn on the radio and read the big red dictionary Miss Ingrid gave me for completing Grade Eight.

The sound of people entering the store cheers me. It isn't the people that make me smile; rather, I find comfort in the slam of the screen door because it is familiar. It sounds like the door at the Chance Hill Tavern. I've noticed how people choose to let the old wooden screen door bang shut behind them even though they could shut it quietly. I think people like being able to make some kind of noticeable sound when given the opportunity.

When it is quiet, I sometimes think of poems that Miss Ingrid taught me. Here is a poem I've been working on writing to capture how I feel as I sit in the store by myself.

"Screen Door Slam"

The crash of the accepting door
echoes in my soul;
I acknowledge no difference
between the people who enter
and extend the same slam of gratitude
as they go.

Do you think I'm fancy for writing poetry in my spare time? The door is worthy of a poem because it creates a rhythm I enjoy. I wonder if Orla's grandfather was made of good stock to be able to build such a decent door.

With Love,
Greta

July 6, 1927

Dear Gertie,

Tonight I met Orla and Martin's son, Walter. Actually, I met Walter when he was a boy and I was a youngster. Sometimes he was at Ellen's house when she cared for me. But I haven't seen Walter since Ellen died when I was three. He brought along his wife, Mabel, and their three-year-old son, Edward.

Walter and Mabel came down from St. Paul for supper. Orla asked me to take a photograph of their family with her new Memo camera. I was embarrassed that she had to instruct me on how to use it. I've never held a camera before.

Walter and Mabel live on Summit Avenue. I asked if they know Mr. Fitzgerald. They asked who he was. I said it was F. Scott Fitzgerald, the man who likes to write books. Walter said, "Oh, Scott. Yes, I met him at the Commodore Hotel once." Walter and Mabel expressed that they were impressed that I knew of Scott. I said that I enjoyed his writing. And they said that perhaps they could show me some of the places he frequented if I wanted to visit them on Summit Avenue.

Walter's and Mabel's acceptance of me caused Orla to look at me differently. Although she thinks she is the cream of the cream, Orla will not like someone or something unless someone she admires expresses admiration for the subject. Sometimes I think Orla is a cow in human skin because she would be lost without a herd to follow.

I did all the cooking and cleaning for Walter and Mabel's visit. Walter said the fried chicken and mashed potatoes I prepared were well paired with the crate of whiskey he brought from St. Paul. I thought whiskey went with everything. Walter said quality whiskey is easy to get at the Commodore Hotel. There is a speakeasy in the basement. The men who work there have connections to Ireland's exports. Orla made a big fuss over the Irish whiskey and said it was a treat to be drinking something other than Kozlowski's Polish moonshine for a change. I said that Summit Avenue must be like

Chance Hill. All the adults laughed. I felt my cheeks turn so crimson that I thought they might burst from the heat. I prayed nobody would notice when my face splattered the table.

(Though I'm so tired, I have to write the conversation that followed on paper, with the hope that it stops spinning in my head and allows me to sleep.) While Orla continued laughing at me, Martin smiled at me and said, "There are similarities to be found between any two things if you look for them long enough."

Orla turned and aimed her piercing laughter at Martin, then said, "I could look until my dying day, and I know I would never find in Chance Hill the opulence that resides on Summit Avenue."

Boldness overcame me, and I spoke directly to Orla. "Material wealth is not something I would consider looking for. The similarity I was referring to was that of acceptance and not having to carry a reputation as a result of activity that some could question."

After my little lecture, Walter set his whiskey glass on the table, clapped, and said, "Bravo, young woman. In that regard, Summit Avenue *is* like Chance Hill."

Orla was no longer laughing. She stared into my eyes. She opened her mouth to speak. After pausing for an uncomfortable amount of time, she closed her mouth, pushed her chair back, stood up, and left the room.

Martin, Walter, and Mabel acted as if there was nothing unusual about her departure. They continued enjoying the meal and making friendly conversation.

Walter is quite attractive; he favors his father in appearance and personality. Martin was raised in Pasadena, California, and I can't help but wonder if that helped make him unlike Orla, who was raised in St. Owen. Walter is studying law at the University of Minnesota. Walter said he wants to practice the kind of law that helps people who can't help themselves. He said he wants everyone to experience the kind of good luck that he has experienced. Orla said she wants her only son to be governor of Minnesota someday and that he should set his sights considerably higher than being a lawyer who wants to help people.

It's odd to imagine someone born in the tiny village of St. Owen possibly being able to run the whole state. Miss Ingrid would say, "That is what makes us America." I like the idea that any dream could possibly come true in this country, as long as it is not ridiculous.

I gave up my room in the attic for Walter and Mabel's visit. It used to be Walter's room when he was a boy. I enjoy the idea of having my own sleeping space that I don't have to share with Matt and Albert. But I'm also happy to give up Walter's old attic room for a night because it overlooks the St. Owen cemetery, and I sometimes hear strange sounds at night.

Do you hear strange sounds where you are?

With Love,
Greta

July 7, 1927

Dear Gertie,

Sweet little Edward wandered out of the bedroom in the middle of the night and cuddled up next to me on the davenport. He stayed with me until I had to get breakfast on. We headed down to the kitchen together. He had great fun counting each step with me as we descended the staircase. It is lovely to see someone else delight in numbers. While we waited for the others to rise for breakfast, I took Edward's photo outside in front of the store. I hesitated to use Orla's camera without her permission. But I was sure she would enjoy having a photo of the sunrise shining on her adorable grandson.

It took quite a long time for the others to wake up. So I moved breakfast to the back of the stove and thought of a way to entertain Edward. I took him to the wall with hardware boxes of fasteners and invited him to scoop handfuls of nuts and bolts into my skirt. We sat at the table for two on the side porch, stacking and counting the nuts and bolts.

Edward enjoyed the simple math I was doing with him. He is

so eager to learn that it makes me want a child of my own to teach. If I had a child, I would teach it everything I know. And then I would teach it how to learn everything that I don't know. I want a child of my own someday even more than my own library filled with books—or maybe I do want both.

Do you think it is fine to have two dreams?

With Love,
Greta

July 8, 1927

Dear Gertie,

Orla and Martin were gone today. They're gone quite a bit because they spend entire days visiting with friends. They frequently visit with friends at the Flynn family's boarding house. I don't blame them for wanting to spend time there. I was there once and saw the fascinating stained-glass windows in the parlor. I could easily spend a day gazing at the Irish images in the glass. The trinity knot is my favorite. Today Orla and Martin were in Freedale all afternoon. So when my duties were completed, and the store wasn't busy, I did a lot of thinking.

I thought about how they were in the same town as Grandma Martha, Matt, and Albert, and they didn't offer to have me ride along. I thought about how the distance they travel each day is typically farther than from St. Owen to Gaston, which Orla said was too far away to drive me to high school.

Next, I thought about how I can use the Pythagorean Theorem to measure the distance between two points on a graph. But in life, the shortest distance between two points can't possibly be a straight line.

I wish my life was two-dimensional so that I could use a theorem to immediately know how to get from here to there. My mind travels that way, and I wish my body could too.

Do you find me silly for sharing such thoughts?

With Love,
Greta

July 10, 1927

Dear Gertie,

Last night I had a dream that I had a baby girl of my own and she brought peace to this world. And she loved me.

Do you think dreams come true?

With Love,
Greta

August 14, 1927

Dear Gertie,

I met Bernard Kozlowski today on his moonshine run to Sweeny's Store. He is handsome and has dark hair and dark eyes. He is more handsome than I am.

Bernard is seventeen, which makes him five years older than me. His family's home is by Lush Lake. I know this because he asked me my age, where I live, and lots of other detailed questions. So I asked him back.

When neither one of us knew what else to say, I offered to help him haul the liquor crates to the dining room, where we have a trap door under the table. We keep a fancy rug on top of the door and pull it back when we want to go down to the secret part of the cellar where we hide the moonshine.

Though it is not easy going down the ladder with a full crate of liquor, I know how to carry a heavy load. Bernard was impressed by my strength and said I was stronger than any chore boy he has ever seen and that he found me to be quite useful.

With Love,
Greta

55

September 2, 1927

Dear Gertie,

I drew on the inside cover of this diary today. The blank space has been begging to be filled ever since Great-Grandma Anna gave me this gift. I filled my time in the store by drawing the Droste can Orla uses to hold her "fun money." Though I've yet to determine how this money is any different than the rest of her money that she enjoys spending, I do admire the illustration on the can. I find it very interesting that the woman on the can is holding a can with her image on it where she is holding a can with her image on it ... It's the only thing I know of that goes on forever.

With Love,
Greta

September 23, 1927

Dear Gertie,

There weren't many customers today, so I read Orla's copy of *New Yorker* magazine. I felt sad when I read a story about finding a good school for children. It sounds as if there are many schools to choose from in New York City. Though I enjoyed Miss Ingrid for a teacher, I regret that I do not live in a city with a choice of schools. Do you think country people deserve a good education? Is there a reason that a good education is reserved for people in certain places?

With Love,
Greta

September 24, 1927

Dear Gertie,

Last night there was rapping outside my window. I thought it might be the ghost of the one-armed Irishman from Chance Hill that I had heard about when I was a child. I heard a beautiful

56

humming sound. So I peered out and saw a bluebird fluttering against the glass. As I admired it, it turned into a beautiful girl who was in her teen years. She looked kind, but I flew back into bed and pulled the bedspread over my head. Who was that?

With Love,
Greta

October 9, 1927

Dear Gertie,

I saw my first talkie yesterday! It was *The Jazz Singer*.

Martin, Orla, and I went to visit Walter, Mabel, and Edward on Summit Avenue in St. Paul. Mabel wanted to see the show again. She had already seen it twice but wanted to see it with us too. It was fabulous to hear Al Jolson's voice on the film. But I'm compelled to see it again because it has caused me to wonder about the practice of smearing black greasepaint on one's face.

We left Edward with Walter and Martin. Then Mabel, Orla, and I went to the Capitol Theater. We rode a streetcar through the city. In the theater I felt I was standing in Jay Gatsby's house because it was so grand. Staircases, marble, chandeliers, fountains, people draped in foreign fabrics ... my head is dizzy with everything I saw in St. Paul.

With Love,
Greta

P.S. Summit Avenue is not like Chance Hill.

October 15, 1927

Dear Gertie,

I went home to visit Ma. Orla and Martin said I should. Wanting to keep my employers happy, I complied with their wishes that I see my mother even though I didn't see the point of it.

The front door to the house seemed smaller than when I left a few months ago, and I wondered if I had grown. I found Ma in the kitchen. I impulsively bent over and embraced her. Orla's touchy ways have been rubbing off on me I suppose. Ma shoved me away. She then told me I was responsible for everything bad that has happened to our family. She threw the Kozlowski jug at me that she had been sipping from. I was happy to discover that I still have good reflexes when I dodged the jug. It crashed into the kitchen wall instead of my head.

As I picked up the broken pieces, and reached for conversation, I told Ma that I met a boy named Bernard Kozlowski. Ma went into a rage and started cussing up a storm. She told me I should stay far away from him if I knew what was good for me. Ma said that those damn slippery Poles were good for nothing. (Except for supplying her with liquor, I would guess.) Ma reached for the butcher knife, and I fled the kitchen before my body could discover what she intended to do with it. I collected my satchel, went out the back door, and ran to the Tavern. Some Engels and some of the Eckmann cousins were there. I had a good time catching up on news with them.

I also met Raymond Redsun. He lives with the Mdewakanton and is the most beautiful man I have ever seen. He knows a lot of people in Chance Hill because his father, John Redsun, and Grandpa Peter Eckmann were friends.

Raymond came over to the table I was sitting at with Cousin Lucille and introduced himself to me. He said he had been stopping by the Tavern often but never saw me there before. I told him that I had recently moved to St. Owen but that my people were from Chance Hill. He asked who I belonged to.

I said that my ma is Berta Hahn Eckmann.

His smile dropped, he put a hand on my shoulder, and said, "I now understand why you have moved away at such a young age."

I wished he would never take his hand off my shoulder because it sent ripples through my body. But he was called over to another table.

Before he walked away, Raymond said it was nice to meet me and that he needed to go do some celebrating. I asked what he was celebrating, and he said, "Life." I've never thought about celebrating life.

When we were done visiting, Cousin Lucille gave me a ride back to St. Owen in her husband's Model T.

With Love,
Greta

P.S. I can't stop thinking about the way it felt when Raymond touched me. Do you think that makes me one of those wayward women Father Richter preaches about?

December 4, 1927

Dear Gertie,

When I told Orla that I was impressed by women who accomplish great things, she announced that she intends to be the first woman in St. Owen who owns a Model A. I wasn't sure if she was trying to be amusing or if she actually expected me to be impressed by the potential of that accomplishment. So I just smiled and nodded politely.

I don't think it was the right response because she stormed out of the room.

With Love,
Greta

January 23, 1928

Dear Gertie,

I read in the newspaper about a man named Hubble who can see beyond the stars that are visible. Do you know what lies beyond the stars? I would like to meet you there someday and be silly once again.

With Love,
Greta

February 1, 1928

Dear Gertie,

Orla rolled in today with her Model A. She calls it "Bonnie." I made a point of making a fuss over how beautiful it is. That was apparently the correct response.

With Love,
Greta

May 13, 1928

Dear Gertie,

Do you think God forgives me for wanting to spend Sundays in the pages of a rational book instead of hearing the repetition of God's Word?

Orla expects me to accompany her and Martin to church every Sunday. Father Collins of St. Owen isn't as awful as Father Richter of St. John's Church. But my mind still drifts toward things of a mathematical and scientific nature when I sit in St. Owen's Church.

If learning about the sciences led me to the discovery of a way to remove all that is evil from humankind's mind, then do you think God would forgive me for wanting to explore the rational world?

With Love,
Greta

June 24, 1928

Dear Gertie,

I think the Church profits from the idea of evil. If the threat of

Hell didn't exist, who would go to church?

With Love,
Greta

July 5, 1928

Dear Gertie,

Yesterday we rode in Bonnie to the Independence Celebration in Northfield. Orla and Martin have new friends there who recently moved from Boston.

Orla had me pack a large picnic and place a sign on the door saying that the store was closed. We made our way to Northfield with Orla driving her great accomplishment. Martin said he was fine with being her passenger.

After meeting up with their friends, we all strolled the street where the James Gang's bank raid had occurred. Then we spent the rest of the day on the banks of the Cannon River. I'm not quite sure why my company was required for the day, other than that Orla might have wanted to show her sophisticated friends that she had a nice car and a servant.

There was nobody my age to speak to, and Orla referred to me a few times as her "girl." In St. Owen she refers to me as the "chore boy." She had me doing unusual tasks for her in front of her friends, such as spreading her skirt when she sat down on the picnic cloth and brushing dust off her backside when she got up. She also had me polish fingerprints off Bonnie where someone had rested a hand on the hood.

It was worth the long day in Northfield and the humiliating situations Orla placed me in when nighttime fell on the city and we saw spectacular fireworks over the Cannon River. It reminded me of that glorious Independence Day that I got to spend with Pa and the boys in New Dresden.

I wonder how the boys celebrated this year. We've spent two Independence Days apart now. I think that I hardly know them anymore.

I'm missing everyone.

With Love,
Greta

August 13, 1928

Dear Gertie,

I won't be starting high school this fall. Orla says she's having far too much fun with me around each day and that life should be fun.

I'm too worn out to try to compel her to think differently. She has proved to be unmovable once her mind is made up.

With Love,
Greta

September 3, 1928

Dear Gertie,

I had a fight with Orla today. When I was evaluating the finances and looking at the investments, I found a gap in the balance. I asked Orla where she and Martin got the funds to invest. She said she borrowed it from her stockbroker and commanded me not to say anything to Martin about it.

I had the strongest feeling that Orla should cash in on her stocks, pay off her broker, and put whatever money was left under the mattress for safe keeping. She demanded to know why I would say something so foolish. I told her I had been monitoring the economic patterns I saw in the newspaper. Sometimes I just know things that I can't explain beyond the patterns that show me what will come next. Orla laughed at me. When she was done laughing, she called me a foolish girl who was raised in a barn by a drunkard. She said since she was not an animal like me, she would do the civilized thing and keep her funds in the stock market.

Do you think my thoughts matter? Do you think thoughts *are* matter that weigh more when they come from certain people?

> With Love,
> Greta

October 13, 1928

Dear Gertie,

That sensation in my arms has returned, and I feel too heavy to move through my days. I have to weep to release the sadness so that I am not so weighed down. At times, I think I'm being swallowed from the inside. Orla has grown weary of my demeanor and told me to stop brooding like my great-uncle did. Puzzled, I asked her to tell me who she was talking about. She said, "Your grandmother Martha's brother Carl, of course." I asked her to tell me more about him. She said there wasn't much to tell because his life ended early with a shot to his head. It happened shortly after Carl and Orla were married.

Why didn't Pa ever tell me about his uncle Carl? Why didn't Ma or Grandma Martha say anything, especially when I announced I should like to work for Carl's former wife and her new husband?

I guess it doesn't surprise me; I seem to care more about family connections than others do. Maybe I like gathering details about my ancestors because it could someday help me understand this unescapable web I feel around me each day.

> With Love,
> Greta

October 15, 1928

Dear Gertie,

The bluebird girl appeared again last night. This time she drew on my window. I leaned closer to the glass pane and saw the faint tracing of *I M A F.*

I'm not sure if I have that correct because, with the hope of deciphering it, I looked down to write it on a scrap of paper. When I looked up again, rain drops had begun to spatter the window pane, and the girl was gone. I don't know how to classify my observations. Can you tell me who she is?

I wish you and I could talk anytime we wanted to.

With Love,
Greta

October 16, 1928

Dear Gertie,

If nobody else can see what I see, do you think that means it isn't real?

With Love,
Greta

October 18, 1928

Dear Gertie,

Do you think it's possible that bits of energy remain after we die that are only detectable by the most sensitive people—and animals? A dog was barking in the cemetery last night. I think it was barking at the girl who visits my window.

With Love,
Greta

October 23, 1928

Dear Gertie,

I asked Martin if he would drive me to Freedale sometime so I could visit Grandma Martha and the boys. He said today was as

64

good as any day. Orla agreed to tend to the store for the afternoon.
So Martin and I left after lunch and were home in time for me to
get supper on. Martin visited friends in town while I visited with
Grandma, Matt, Albert, and the aunts.

I told Grandma I recently found out that her brother had been
married to Orla. I felt as if I had cussed in front of Grandma because
she went pale and silent. I told her I didn't mean to upset her by
mentioning Carl. She said that was fine and that she was surprised
that she still missed him so much. She said she misses Pa a lot too. I
held her while she mourned her brother and son. Then she started
crying about her five younger siblings that died from a disease almost
fifty years ago. I've never heard about them before. That is a long
time to be sad about losing someone.

I had a good visit with the boys before they ran off to play with
friends. They struggle to live among three old women in such a
tiny house now that all the cousins have moved on. But they enjoy
attending school in Freedale with the town kids. I'm happy about
their situation.

With Love,
Greta

November 6, 1928

Dear Gertie,

I wish I was old enough to vote. I like Alfred Smith. He's
Catholic and against Prohibition. I can't wait to vote. I don't
understand why more women don't do it.

Orla enjoys exercising her right to say who should be in power.
I'm tempted to think she writes her own name on the ballot. But she
claims she is voting for Herbert Hoover because he wants to put a
chicken in every pot and a car in every garage. I guess Orla believes
that it is important to vote for having more than she actually needs.

With Love,
Greta

November 20, 1928

Dear Gertie,

Orla is finally done being angry at me for suggesting that she cash in on her stocks. She drove me to St. Paul to see *Steamboat Willie* with her, Mabel, and Edward. It was very enjoyable. It was also enjoyable to watch Edward enjoying the cartoon. He did a good job of sitting still during *Gang War*, the film that followed the Mickey Mouse film. For being so well-behaved, Orla insisted on rewarding Edward with an ice cream cone afterward. Edward insisted on sitting next to me at the café so he could teach me how to sound like Mickey Mouse. He is very clever for a four-year-old.

With Love,
Greta

February 2, 1929

Dear Gertie,

Do you think thoughts become energy once they are formed in the brain? It must take energy to form them, and I don't think energy goes away.

Do you think our world would feel different if we all had good thoughts?

With Love,
Greta

April 30, 1929

Dear Gertie,

Orla is quite beside herself. Her broker called in his loans. She has nothing left for personal savings and is blaming me for it because I keep the books. I overheard her telling Martin it was my fault. I could tell by his response that he didn't believe her. Martin isn't a stupid man and knew her ways with money long before I came along. He said he had some money tucked away that will see them through. She asked where it was. When Martin wouldn't tell her, she stormed out of the house in a rage.

With Love,
Greta

June 15, 1929

Dear Gertie,

Orla must have persuaded Martin to share some of his funds because she reinvested quite a sum in the stock market through a new broker. It tied my stomach in a knot when I discovered it. Orla seems to think securities will advance forever. Perhaps she hasn't experienced enough hardship to know that nothing good lasts forever.

With Love,
Greta

August 14, 1929

Dear Gertie,

I wish I had time to read a novel. I wish that you and I were characters in a novel and that I was the author so I could write my way to you.

With Love,
Greta

November 1, 1929

Dear Gertie,

Orla lost all that she had invested of Martin's money in stocks. She turned to me and asked how I, as the bookkeeper, could have allowed that to happen. There were so many words that sprung to my mind that they got tangled together, and I couldn't say anything.

With Love,
Greta

February 15, 1930

Dear Gertie,

People around here sure are tightening their purse strings. When customers come to the store, they buy the smallest quantity possible out of fear of overinvesting in too much of anything—even flour and sugar.

With Love,
Greta

April 23, 1930

Dear Gertie,

This spring, Bernard Kozlowski has been stopping by regularly with small moonshine deliveries. I hadn't seen him for quite some time because one of his older brothers was delivering for our route. Flour and sugar are unaffordable to most customers now. But those same customers have the funds for a bit of likker. I don't fault them because everyone needs a little relief. The Kozlowski's business seems to be the only one that is faring well in this area. They actually expanded their delivery area because their product is superior to that of other moonshiners. Maybe I'll ask Bernard what the secret method is to making their product.

As we were storing the moonshine under the floor, I thought about commenting to Bernard that if he were to bring more moonshine with each trip, he could come by less frequently. I thought better of it because he is a man; it would be improper for a girl to offer advice on conducting business.

With Love,
Greta

April 24, 1930

Dear Gertie,

Last night a white spider descended from the ceiling above my bed. You know my hatred for spiders and that, typically, I would have disposed of it. But I am so lonely for companionship that I didn't bother it. I watched it spin a web from my bed post to the wall until I fell asleep.

This morning I looked at the web, and the spider was gone. It may be in my hair for all I know, and I don't even mind if it is.

I don't think I will brush my hair today.

With Love,
Greta

July 30, 1930

Dear Gertie,

The crops around here are not looking good. They're starting to shrivel as a blanket of despair seems to have fallen on everything. I find myself wondering if we will all just silently wither away like the cornstalks or if God (otherwise known as "rain") will eventually intervene.

Do you still believe in God?

With Love,
Greta

October 8, 1930

Dear Gertie,

Locals are calling alcohol by a new name because of me. Since a Prohibition agent has been on the prowl lately, and customers have been requesting the smallest quantity they can buy, I convinced Martin and Orla that we should keep a jug of moonshine in the sugar barrel by the counter. Other shops in this area have gotten caught in a trap with the agent posing as an honest customer seeking a drink. So I've instructed all our regular customers who stop in to call likker "a bit of sugar" and to bring in a flask that can be concealed before they go out the door. I've put a stack of books on the counter in front of the sugar barrel (which I actually hope to read sometime) so that when people request "a bit of sugar" and slip me their flasks, I can discreetly fill the customers' orders.

If people actually want sugar for baking, they request "cake sugar." Then I go to a barrel marked Likker where we keep the sugar we sell. I recently painted the barrel and made the lettering look as if it was from before Prohibiton started more than ten years ago. I thought that if an agent does come in the store, he would go straight to the Likker barrel, see that it's filled with sugar, and give up the search because the barrel is old-looking. If an agent does inspect the sugar barrel where I keep the alcohol, he will lift the lid and see that it appears to be full of sugar. I used Martin's tools to build a false bottom into the barrel that has sugar sitting on top of it. I cut a small removable section out of the side of the barrel at the bottom to retrieve the Kozlowski jugs that are stored in the lower part.

Martin has joked that former Congressman Andrew Volstead would make sauerkraut illegal if he could. He said to me that if Mr. Volstead decides to tour the Minnesota countryside and drop by to see if we are abiding by his beloved Prohibition Act, I must tell him all I know about the ill effects of taking intoxicating liquor—which I know inside and out. I will tell him in full detail about Ma. That should convince him that I must be a teetotaler like him and would never consider selling liquor. It would be a lie, of course. Some might call me a scofflaw for my behavior. But I would much rather serve the residents of St. Owen Kozlowski's trusted moonshine from our store than have them purchase someone else's bad batch that has been cut with paint thinner. Those who need a drink will manage to find it anywhere. I think the best way to make someone want something is to make it illegal.

I'm thankful for my ability to hide things. I believe my rigged sugar barrel is the first thing I've done that has impressed Orla because she said to me, "Having a drunkard for a mother has taught you something useful."

With Love,
Greta

October 9, 1930

Dear Gertie,

The government should make reading illegal, then we would become a nation of secret readers, and the demand for books would increase. The resulting supply could make it more affordable for me to someday own as many books as I want.

With Love,
Greta

January 6, 1931

Dear Gertie,

I have been failing to write you.

Orla is rationing our meals, and my energy is quite low. I make sure Orla and Martin get substantially more than I get to eat. I don't want to eat my share and cause them to be excessively hungry. I want to avoid knowing how terrible Orla's mood might be in a state of starvation.

When I sit with the intention to write, I immediately fall asleep because, it seems, the act of composing thoughts is too taxing for my body.

With Love,
Greta

May 5, 1931

Dear Gertie,

Bernard asked if I would marry him someday. I was quite

surprised. He had previously indicated no interest in me that I could detect. Mostly, he has treated me as he would treat a chore boy. I responded that I was only sixteen and would still like to get my high school education. He asked if I would promise to marry him when I felt old and educated enough. I thanked him and told him I would consider it.

Though I didn't say so to him, I am bothered that Bernard only has a fifth-grade education and seems to have no desire to learn anything more. I've been given reason in the past to wonder whether he can read.

With Love,
Greta

July 19, 1931

Dear Gertie,

I experienced good fortune today. Orla and Martin were attending a funeral in Northfield when Bernard stopped by with the moonshine. I helped him carry it to the dining room, and we stored it under the floor. Since there had been no customers while Bernard was with me, he asked if I wanted to help him with the rest of his deliveries. Orla and Martin planned to be gone until tomorrow, and all our regular customers had already stopped by. So I put a Closed sign in the window and said I would ride along with Bernard because I was in the mood for new scenery.

After we made the final delivery in Rottenburg, Bernard asked if I would like to go to Lush Lake and go shore fishing with him. I said I would. He asked if I wanted to see how fast his horses could go. I said I did. Bernard said he would need to remove the extra weight from the wagon so that I could experience his team at top speed. So I helped him lift the empty jugs and the crates that held the remaining full jugs into the overgrown ditch. We got back on the wagon, and he instructed me to hold on tight. As soon as he got the team up to a good trot, we heard the horn of a model A. It was a Prohibition agent. Bernard stopped the horses and the agent proceeded to do a thorough inspection of the wagon—which had, thankfully, been emptied of every evidence of moonshine. Had the agent stopped us five minutes earlier, I might be writing you from jail right now.

We spent most of the afternoon fishing. When Bernard was returning me to the store, I offered to help him reload the wagon. He said he didn't want to risk getting me into trouble, and he would collect the jugs and crates after delivering me to the store.

Bernard Kozlowski seems like a decent enough man.

With Love,
Greta

August 2, 1931

Dear Gertie,

Yesterday Orla sold Bonnie to a wealthy man from Mankato so she could buy more food for Martin and herself. She has been inconsolable. Though I've tried to bring her appealing meals, she would rather cry into her pillow than eat. I don't really mind her troubled state. Her lack of appetite means I get to eat the food she refuses.

Do you think I should let this routine continue, or should I tell Orla to stop behaving like her first husband, who died from a shot to his head?

With Love,
Greta

August 24, 1931

Dear Gertie,

That ghostly bluebird girl appeared outside my window again last night. She said to me, "Subtract the sum from the chosen number." When she was done talking, she stepped into my side of the window and danced with me. I spun around and shut my eyes to fully enjoy the dancing. When I opened my eyes, she was gone.

So I was unable to ask her what she means by her instructions. I believe it is only part of a silly riddle. The next time I see her I will ask her to explain her math to me.

With Love,
Greta

August 25, 1931

Dear Gertie,

"Subtract the sum from the chosen number."

With Love,
Greta

August 26, 1931

Dear Gertie,

"Subtract the sum from the chosen number."

With Love,
Greta

August 27, 1931

Dear Gertie,

"Subtract the sum from the chosen number." No matter how many times I write it, it still means nothing to me. Though I don't believe in ghosts, the real sensation brought about by my encounter with the ghost girl at my window agrees with my sense of reason. Do you think that makes her real?

With Love,
Greta

74

August 28, 1931

Dear Gertie,

If ghosts can address mathematics, can mathematics address ghosts?

With Love,
Greta

August 29, 1931

Dear Gertie,

I wish I knew the dimensions of my mind so that I could graph its contents. Maybe then I would understand the ghost girl. Though I haven't seen her for five days, her mathematical instruction occupies the front of my mind.

Do you suppose she is addressing the deficient state of affairs I find myself in, or is she simply speaking the predictable language of bookkeeping? Though I've enjoyed riddles in the past, this one seems so important that it would be simply beautiful if I could find the answer.

With Love,
Greta

September 9, 1931

Dear Gertie,

Orla announced that she and Martin will be selling the store and moving to St. Paul to live with Walter, Mabel, and Edward. They can't afford to keep me. Orla said I will have to find my own way or move into a Hooverville. She pointed out that Bernard has an eye for me. I said I was aware of that and told her he asked for my hand a while ago.

Orla advised me to marry him.

With Love,
Greta

September 17, 1931

Dear Gertie,

Who do you think I'll become next? First, I was Berta Eckmann's daughter, then I was Orla Beach's chore boy, and I don't know who I'll belong to next.

Who do you think I would be if I belonged only to me?

With Love,
Greta

October 18, 1931

Dear Gertie,

This morning, I saw a white raven sitting on the Flynn gravestone at the corner of the cemetery. I sensed that the raven wanted to carry me away, so I ran inside the store.

I stayed inside all day and helped Orla and Martin pack their belongings into trunks and old moonshine crates. For someone who can't afford to keep me, Orla has a lot of belongings to pack.

With Love,
Greta

November 2, 1931

Dear Gertie,

As they handed the keys to the general store over to the owner of the New Dresden Creamery, my farewell to Orla and Martin was lacking in emotion. Though I will miss Martin, and I think he will miss my company, neither of us dared express that sentiment in Orla's presence. I felt nothing concerning parting ways with Orla; I expect she felt the same because, from her perspective, I was only a hired chore boy.

There was an equal lack of emotion exchanged when I informed Bernard that I would be willing to marry him if the offer was still on the table. Getting married is the practical thing to do. Grandma Martha and my aunts don't have the funds or the space to provide for me along with my brothers. And Bernard needs someone to cook and clean for him in his empty house.

With Love,
Greta

November 4, 1931

Dear Gertie,

I married Bernard yesterday. I wish you could have been at my wedding. The ceremony was at St. Adalbert's church on Lush Lake, and Father Wójcik did the ceremony. The church Bernard's grandfather helped build is one of the grandest Catholic churches in this area. It has the most colorful Stations of the Cross that I've ever seen. Bernard's mother freshens up the paint on them each year before Lent. The thirteenth station is my favorite one because Bernard's mother has Mary's face so painted up that she looks like a clown.

Bernard's father, Johnny, gets along with me fine. But Bernard's mother, Ludmila, doesn't like me. Though I try to be my best around her, I suspect she doesn't like me because I'm not Polish. Most of the people in attendance at our wedding were Bernard's Polish family and friends. Although I invited Ma to the wedding, she said she was busy. I was thankful that Grandma Martha, Matt, and Albert were there so that I had someone to speak to in a language I could understand. Almost everyone around us was speaking Polish even though they also know English. In some situations I find that rude—and my wedding day would be one of those situations. I'm trying to forgive their ignorance.

A neighbor of Bernard's family named Agnieszka was my attendant who signed our marriage license as a witness. Everyone seems to like her. She doesn't seem to like me. She grew up next to Bernard's family farm and is slightly older than him. Her husband died last month. Bernard calls her Aggie. She has very light—almost white—hair, pale blue eyes, and the fairest skin I've ever seen. She touches Bernard's forearm a lot when she talks with us. She hasn't touched me yet. Maybe it will just take time for her to get to know I'm a decent person, then we can be friends. Since Bernard really seems to enjoy her, I'm sure I will eventually enjoy her company too.

Bernard was given a piece of his father's land near Lush Lake, and he planted crops on it this spring. For our wedding gift, Bernard's folks said that next spring they would give us a hen, rooster, and chicks to raise. Bernard has a little shack on the farmland, and it's my home now. When I used to think about what my adult home would be like, it wasn't like this.

For our honeymoon, I asked Bernard if we could go to Mankato and rent a room at the Mount Kato Inn. Orla had suggested that it would be an enjoyable destination. Bernard said that would be a stupid waste of money when we have a good bed right here. I don't think I would call it a good bed. It's an old mattress from Bernard's folks that has hard lumps, and it sits on top of an old box spring that creaks with every movement. The frame wobbles and causes me to wonder if I should wrap a pillow around my head to protect it when Bernard and I eventually crash to the floor.

Perhaps I should go without a pillow; the resulting brain damage might help me survive this questionable adventure I've embarked on.

With Love,
Greta

November 8, 1931

Dear Gertie,

Going to Mass is very important to Bernard's family. When we went this morning, Aggie showed up late and sat in our pew, right next to Bernard. I noticed that his knees were turned toward her. For some reason that bothered me.

With Love,
Greta

November 15, 1931

Dear Gertie,

I wonder if I'm the only Prussian descendant at St. Adalbert's church. I don't care that they're mostly Polish. But many of them seem to care very much that I'm of German heritage. When I lived in St. Owen, nobody seemed to care where my family came from or which languages I knew.

As I sat in church, instead of listening to the priest drone on in Latin, I thought in German about how I didn't think I would be married at age sixteen.

I will be sure to make a point of getting my high school education now that I am a married woman in charge of my life.

With Love,
Greta

November 16, 1931

Dear Gertie,

This morning I made breakfast for Bernard with eggs and bacon that Grandma Martha gave to us for a wedding gift. Bernard took one look at the plate I set in front of him, stood up, picked up the bacon, and tossed it in the slop bucket.

I don't know if I'm more disturbed by the contemptuous look he gave me or that I considered retrieving the bacon from the slop because I'm so hungry.

Why would anyone despise bacon?

With Love,
Greta

November 23, 1931

Dear Gertie,

Why do you suppose Bernard thinks it's his right to decide what I want? If I tell him I don't want something as trivial as more milk in my glass, he says that I do. If I argue with him, he tells me I don't know anything.

I wonder what Miss Ingrid would think of the way Bernard governs this home with ignorance instead of knowledge. Maybe this is a "Prologue to a Farce or a Tragedy; or, perhaps both."

With Love,
Greta

December 2, 1931

Dear Gertie,

Although it's been more difficult than ever to find time to write, some things simply *beg* to be written. In my limited free time, when Bernard lets me take his buckboard, I've been going to the Middleton Café where there's a copy of the *St. Paul Daily Globe*. I've promised a steady supply of eggs next year to the owner, Helga, in exchange for letting me sit at a table and catch up on the news. She said she'll save back issues for me to take home if I can't stop by much in the winter.

Although I don't mean to be disrespectful to President Hoover, I must say I don't understand why he is fueling trade wars. I believe that will only continue to hurt our economy. I think he should make a point of investing in science. I think that is something that would give back to our country in so many ways.

Since our future chickens will provide eggs for me to trade for knowledge, I finally feel grateful for the brood Bernard's parents promised us. I've been informed that I will have to tend to their care because Bernard says it's women's work—and that he doesn't care for chicken shit. Who does? We currently milk seven cows each day and the creamery picks up our cans on the way to bigger farms instead of us having to haul them. I wish we had to haul the milk cans so I could get into town more often.

With Love,
Greta

December 3, 1931

Dear Gertie,

You would be surprised to see that my hands look like a man's now because of all the wood chopping I've been doing. Do you remember how we used to stare at our hands and decide what God made them for? Your hands were for picking blue flowers and mine were made for holding books. You were going to grow cornflower bouquets. And I was going to be someone who held books for others when I grew up. Am I grown up yet?

Do you remember talking about the many books I would someday hold? I still dream of having a library of my own. Most people around these parts still find it frivolous to throw away good money on books. I've given up trying to convey that I think the value of some things simply can't be measured in dollars. I've saved every book and magazine ever given to me. Because of Bernard's preference for the goose fat his mother used in her baking and cooking, I keep my reading materials stowed in the back of the pantry behind the lard Grandma Martha has given me. Bernard won't stumble on them there and use them for kindling the fire in the cookstove. Bernard doesn't view books in the same way I do. He doesn't see a lot of things in the way I do. I believe our differences are vast enough to fill every shelf in the Library of Congress.

With Love,
Greta

December 4, 1931

Dear Gertie,

Now my hands are also being used to make moonshine.

Bernard and his brothers have been teaching me their distilling process. Two of his brothers have pushed their bodies against mine while instructing me. I don't think it was accidental. I feel sick to my stomach as I write about it. But I also wonder if a good wife is supposed to let her husband's brothers touch her body. Bernard saw it happen both times and didn't say anything.

The brothers rigged a still in our hayloft. We have to keep it dismantled when it's not in use, in case Prohibition agents stop by. I helped pick out the perfect tree branches on our property to hide the coils.

Right after we got married, Bernard made it my job to bury his share of the moonshine he and his brothers sell. When the ground was still warm enough, I dug several holes around the yard to store the jugs and discovered that I excel at finding ways to conceal holes. My favorite cover is a corn sheller. It stands on top of old boards that appear to be there to balance the lop-sided frame of the sheller. But the random-appearing boards are actually attached to a hinged lid underneath that I constructed. I secured the corn sheller legs to the boards in such a way that we simply need to pull the crank backward to tip open the lid and reveal the jugs below ground. It was enjoyable to use my hands for making that clever contraption.

With Love,
Greta

December 5, 1931

Dear Gertie,

We finally finished harvesting the corn that Bernard and his father planted on this farm. Marriage seems to come with plenty to do, and I've had no trouble falling asleep at night. Sometimes I wish I could stay up and see if the girl from St. Owen followed me here.

With Love,
Greta

December 10, 1931

Dear Gertie,

Thursdays are especially busy for me. Bernard goes ice fishing on Lush Lake with his brothers all day so that we can have fish on Fridays.

I've never cared for fish and have already grown quite tired of eating sunnies and bullheads. I don't really care for being Catholic on Fridays. Or Saturday through Thursday.

With Love,
Greta

February 13, 1932

Dear Gertie,

All the women of St. Adalbert's Church have to take turns cleaning the church each month. I'm with the women that do it every second Saturday morning. I work with five other women dusting and polishing the church from top to bottom.

There is a lot more cleaning to be had in St. Adalbert's than most Catholic churches around here because of all the ornate statues with long Polish words carved into them that catch dust. It's my job to clean the pews. The other women take care of everything else. I don't know their names. I introduced myself, and they laughed at me, handed me a dust rag, then pointed to the pews.

Today I thought about math while I dusted. I imagined that the polished wood was a chalkboard. With my mind, I wrote algebraic equations with sigma notation on the pews, then erased them with my polishing rag. It made me happy in the moment.

With Love,
Greta

May 20, 1932

Dear Gertie,

Did you hear that Amelia Earhart flew across the Atlantic Ocean by herself?

And here is more grand news: I think I'm expecting! If it's a girl, I hope she becomes a pilot one day. I want her to be free to fly and see this world.

I will make a point of teaching her English and German, and I might learn to speak Polish with her.

With Love,
Greta

May 30, 1932

Dear Gertie,

The wild flowers that came up along the driveway bring me such joy.

With Love,
Greta

June 6, 1932

Dear Gertie,

Bernard ran over my flowers today.

With Love,
Greta

June 14, 1932

Dear Gertie,

It appears that I'm not pregnant. It's just as well. I don't know how I would have time to properly care for a child when I can't seem to care for myself. I know that I must not look very attractive because I often find Bernard's eyes resting on other women's bodies in church.

With Love,
Greta

July 4, 1932

Dear Gertie,

Bernard's family had a party on the shores of Lush Lake. I've never owned a proper swimming suit, so Aggie offered me her old one. I said it wasn't necessary. I didn't want to explain my dislike of the water so, when she persisted, I simply said, "No, thank you."

Bernard said I was being rude and that I should take the suit and put it on. I obeyed my husband and took the outfit from the most voluptuous Aggie. Though I didn't see myself in a mirror, I could tell the suit hung on me as if I were a scarecrow. When I approached the group, Aggie smiled broadly and told me I looked swell. I knew it was a line. Bernard's sisters Stacia and Marcie were snickering behind my back.

Bernard told me to get in his boat so we could go fishing. I told him no, without going into detail concerning my refusal. Bernard threw his hands in the air. He grabbed his fishing pole and walked toward the boat. Aggie called after him and said she was up for fishing. He smiled at her and motioned for her to get in his boat. Bernard and Aggie spent the afternoon on the water while I sat on the shore in Aggie's floppy swimming suit. I sat there while watching Bernard's family get zozzled on their moonshine. And I ate the entire bowl of German potato salad I brought to the picnic because nobody else would eat it.

How was your Independence Day?

With Love,
Greta

August 12, 1932

Dear Gertie,

I thought of another good thing about not having a child. If I had one, I can't imagine having any time at all to write to you. With the caring for the chickens, milking the cows, gardening, tending to the stills, making breakfast, doing dishes, baking bread, doing dishes, making dinner, doing dishes, doing laundry, ironing, making supper, doing dishes, attending church, cleaning church, weekly card parties with Bernard's family ... I barely have a moment to jot the occasional thought to share with you. These hands are filled with dishes and other chores and haven't held a book in a long while—other than this one I am writing for you.

With Love,
Greta

P.S. I despise doing dishes.

October 19, 1932

Dear Gertie,

On the way home from church last Sunday, I started crying. Bernard asked what the hell was wrong with me. I told him I felt sick. But I was crying because Bernard was staring at Aggie in church. For some reason his gazing at her sticks like a rod through my heart. If he's married to me, why are his eyes resting on her? Did I imagine that he was looking at her and blushing? If he was looking at her, is it because I'm not enough to look at? If I caught a married man gazing at me the way Bernard gazes at Aggie, I think I would gouge his eyes out of his sockets and hand them to his wife. Why do you suppose Aggie won't do that for me?

Why do you suppose I can't stop crying about the way he gazes at her?

With Love,
Greta

October 21, 1932

Dear Gertie,

When Bernard looks into my eyes I feel replaceable.
Do you think all married women feel that way?

With Love,
Greta

November 3, 1932

Dear Gertie,

Bernard and I have been married one year. I had no idea marriage would make me so homely. Orla's magazines didn't mention that about married women.

Last week, when Bernard seemed in a pleasant mood after having his way with me, I impulsively asked him if he thought I was pretty. He laughed loud and hard. When he was done laughing, he said to me, "You'll never be pretty. You're too tall to be pretty." A lump appeared in my throat that was bigger than any I've felt before. I still haven't quite swallowed it.

Do you think a piece of my soul got knocked loose and is stuck in my throat?

With Love,
Greta

November 4, 1932

Dear Gertie,

Do you think I lack beauty for Bernard to see, or does he simply have unseeing eyes?

With Love,
Greta

November 15, 1932

Dear Gertie,

The neighbor men, who were helping Bernard with the threshing, were dreaming out loud about someday buying an International Harvester diesel engine tractor. I'm starting to pray that God will give Bernard a tractor like that. I'm making note of the date I start praying about it because I want to discover how long it takes God to answer a prayer.

With Love,
Greta

December 8, 1932

Dear Gertie,

Last night I smelled perfume on Bernard's shirt when he came home from the men's church meeting. I know it wasn't mine because we can't afford perfume. He was smiling too; Bernard usually only smiles when he's drinking with his brothers and playing cards.

Maybe I'll stop praying that God will reward Bernard with a tractor.

With Love,
Greta

December 9, 1932

Dear Gertie,

My arms are so heavy. I don't know how I'll get the potatoes peeled tonight. My feet are heavy too.

With Love,
Greta

December 15, 1932

Dear Gertie,

Last night I went to the women's meeting at church. Aggie was there. I recognized the scent of her perfume.

I don't think I will brush my hair today.

With Love,
Greta

January 4, 1933

Dear Gertie,

Do you know what love is? I'm not sure that I do—besides what I feel for you. Do you think love can be measured?

With Love,
Greta

February 13, 1933

Dear Gertie,

Bernard raised his fist at me tonight. He didn't punch me though. I shouldn't have provoked him by telling him that I still dream of going to high school and doing something with my life.

Some things are best kept secret.

With Love,
Greta

May 5, 1933

Dear Gertie,

I wish I had someone to really talk to, other than you. Some of the women at St. Adalbert's are starting to be decent to me because I have learned enough Polish to make polite conversation. But they make it clear that I'll never be accepted as one of them.

We see Bernard's family at least two times a week with church doings and blackjack card parties to attend. Johnny and Ludmila moved to New Dresden, and their new home is big enough to have several blackjack tables set up. None of Bernard's family seems able to keep track of the cards in the way I do. But I'm learning how not to win too frequently so as to avoid their ire. I've actually begun to find enjoyment in not winning because it is such a challenge to lose to the Kozlowskis. They play for money. Bernard and I could greatly increase our take home pot if I allowed myself to play to my best ability. But then the Kozlowski pot of cruelty for me would overflow.

On occasion it's worth my time to attend parties when I can use my winnings to pay Bernard's folks to use their telephone to call Grandma Martha in Freedale. I wish we had phone lines running to our house. Talking to Grandma Martha and the boys helps make time go by. When I'm not talking to anyone, the space I'm in still feels stationary.

Do you think life is meant to move?

With Love,
Greta

June 2, 1933

Dear Gertie,

Helga at the Middleton Café has been making a point of visiting with me at length when I drop off the eggs. She's lonely because her husband passed away. I don't mind that I don't have time to read the news when I'm there because giving Helga my time makes her feel good.

How do you think I would react if Bernard passed away?

With Love,
Greta

June 27, 1933

Dear Gertie,

I'm starting to look forward to card parties at Bernard's folks' house. They've started playing *National Barn Dance* on the radio while we're there. Although I still prefer the sound of Wagner, I also enjoy hearing Gene Autry sing. Hearing him croon helps me forget about my life for a moment.

I wish Bernard would be willing to buy a radio for me so that I could forget about life all the time.

With Love,
Greta

September 9, 1933

Dear Gertie,

Do you ever think about doing life over? If so, how would you do it? I would be born in a town or a city so that I could go to school through Grade Twelve. I would have a Ma and a Pa who enjoyed reading the newspaper and listening to a radio so they could stay current, and we would enjoy traveling the world together. I would go to college and study math at a place where women are allowed to learn. I would walk among people who found me useful.

I overheard Bernard's family murmuring about why we don't have children yet. It seems they question my usefulness because I'm not producing another little bootlegger to carry on the Kozlowski name.

I don't know what I'm doing wrong. I let Bernard have his way with me whenever he wants. I've even gotten to the point where I don't picture Aggie when he's on top of me. I think about what's beyond the stars instead of what is inside me.

With Love,
Greta

December 6, 1933

Dear Gertie,

Prohibition is officially over! There is talk that we could someday soon go into a store filled with beer and liquor and buy a variety to take home instead of having to make it or purchase it on the sly. Just imagine what that world would be like! I wonder what this will do to the business that Bernard and his brothers have made for themselves.

With Love,
Greta

December 19, 1933

Dear Gertie,

After coming down from a two week bender, Bernard is in quite a mood. Though he doesn't have sufficient words to convey his thoughts, I suspect he is afraid of the financial changes that are coming.

I will increase the flock of hens to seventy-five and start selling eggs and butchered chickens to help bring in some money to replace what will be lost through decreased moonshine sales.

With Love,
Greta

January 12, 1934

Dear Gertie,

I've had more time to read the newspaper at the Middleton Café lately because Helga isn't so lonely anymore. She found another man to take her mind off her sadness. I can't even imagine what man would be strong enough to lift my mind off my sadness.

With Love,
Greta

February 2, 1934

Dear Gertie,

Albert Einstein visited the White House last week. I wish I could have witnessed the conversation between him and President Roosevelt. This country is fortunate to have Einstein here. I think that America could move forward a great distance if the government was fueled by the brain power found in the heads of men and women like Einstein.

With Love,
Greta

May 17, 1934

Dear Gertie,

FDR's New Deal seems to be helping the country a bit. When I go into Middleton, people are often caught smiling. Some of the children are becoming plump. Men are finding work at factories in the big cities and are able to better provide for their families. I wish Bernard would consider a job in the city so we could move there.

With Love,
Greta

June 24, 1934

Dear Gertie,

I am so sorry. Where have the days gone? I failed to do a novena for you this month. I am beside myself because there aren't enough days left in June to make it up. I'm filled with guilt. Please, do you forgive me? I have been so exhausted at night that I'm asleep almost before my head touches the pillow. I must have gotten out of the habit at some point.

With Love,
Greta

July 24, 1934

Dear Gertie,

I'm troubled by how power is abused by some men. Yesterday I read in the newspaper about Minneapolis policemen opening fire on a truck full of picketers who had no weapons. They presented harm to nobody; however, threat was felt by employers who over-profit from the picketers' labor. It was a truck full of truck drivers seeking better work conditions. They were only armed with dangerous voices that demanded fair treatment.

Are you afraid of men with power?

With Love,
Greta

September 22, 1934

Dear Gertie,

I hope that the life I'm living someday converges with the life I want.

With Love,
Greta

November 7, 1934

Dear Gertie,

Why do you suppose I continue to fail to get pregnant? What am I doing wrong?

With Love,
Greta

January 27, 1935

Dear Gertie,

Do you think life would be better if I had continued the habit of praying the novena?

With Love,
Greta

February 19, 1935

Dear Gertie,

I borrowed Johnny and Ludmila's Chevy today so I could visit Grandma Martha in Freedale. The boys and the aunts weren't there. But Grandma and I had a nice visit while we ate bacon sandwiches.

Grandma is starting to fade, so I'm happy I was able to see her. I couldn't help but feel sad as I drove back to New Dresden to return the auto to Bernard's parents. I was hoping that Grandma would have at least remembered to wish me "Happy Birthday." Nobody remembered my birthday today.

With Love,
Greta

April 8, 1935

Dear Gertie,

We had a runner today. Bernard missed the chicken's jugular vein, and she ran around the yard with her head dangling from her neck for a good eight hours. At first we tried catching her so Bernard could axe her again. But she kept slipping away. We decided to just wait it out and pick her up when she was done running. She didn't stop until after supper. I wish she would have had the brains to run down the driveway and disappear from here so that she wouldn't end up on tomorrow night's dinner table.

What kept her here?

With Love,
Greta

July 14, 1935

Dear Gertie,

I wonder if a ray of light goes in search of other worlds indefinitely. I'm missing you.

Do you miss me?

With Love,
Greta

October 30, 1935

Dear Gertie,

Bernard built a little shed next to the barn. People come over here and he butchers their animals for them. I enjoy the company that stops by, despite the blood and guts I have to wash out of Bernard's clothes each night.

With Love,
Greta

March 28, 1936

Dear Gertie,

Adolf Hitler's troops are occupying Rhineland. I fear that Prussian relatives are being killed by Hitler. Do you think anyone in America cares?

With Love,
Greta

August 21, 1936

Dear Gertie,

I find myself pondering whether the principle of causation is lost on American leaders. I'm furious that the United States didn't boycott the Olympics in Berlin. If this country can't make a stand for the humane treatment of all humans, it doesn't deserve to hold such a powerful place in the world's eyes.

With Love,
Greta

August 29, 1936

Dear Gertie,

Support of Adolf Hitler's antics will only hurt this nation for decades. But many of the Christians I know seem indifferent to the suffering of the Jews.

Why do you think Jews are so hated? What is it that greedy men fear will be taken from them by Jews?

With Love,
Greta

October 31, 1936

Dear Gertie,

There is a general fighting in Spain's Civil War named Francisco Franco. He is obsessed with putting his nation first, above all else, and I find myself obsessed with him. He wants all Spaniards to think what the Nationalists think, or he will destroy them. I'm grateful that America is a democracy and that my country doesn't have to tolerate that kind of leader.

With Love,
Greta

November 2, 1936

Dear Gertie,

Adolf Hitler from Germany and Benito Mussolini from Italy are supporting Franco. I know of many American Catholics who are supporting him too. I struggle to understand how it is that the same people who claim to desire to do God's will also desire to support a leader who hurts people for thinking differently than he does. Maybe being victorious at promoting their version of religion is more important to them than succeeding at protecting fellow human beings from harm. Maybe my God desires more kindness among people than theirs does.

With Love,
Greta

November 4, 1936

Dear Gertie,

I voted! I helped re-elect Franklin Delano Roosevelt. It probably was not as big of a deal to him as it was to me that I helped; it was my first time in the voting booth. When I filled out my ballot, I felt what I think would be called "power." I'm not sure because I've never had that feeling before.

Although I detest his foreign policies, I like FDR's New Deal ideas. I believe they will eventually make our country prosperous.

Sometimes I wish I could run the country. How long do you think it will be until this country elects a woman president?

With Love,
Greta

February 19, 1937

Dear Gertie,

I'm twenty-two years old today. Do you think I'm too old to go to high school? At what point is a dream dead?

When do you think it's best not to pursue a dream in the first place?

With Love,
Greta

July 3, 1937

Dear Gertie,

I'm tempted to tell Bernard that I refuse to sit by Lush Lake with his family tomorrow. After weighing the benefits and costs of doing so, I am opting for silence. When I don't perform as he desires me to, Bernard releases daggers from his eyes that are far more threatening than the butcher knives he wields.

Bernard has cut me into so many small pieces over the years that I don't know if I can survive being made any smaller. So my thoughts are best kept locked up. There is considerable silence in this home. I often find myself wishing the bluebird ghost girl from St. Owen would return because, despite her nonsensical nature, she desired to communicate with me.

Lately, I find myself engaging in imaginary conversations with Bernard about "independence" and whether it should be celebrated in this country.

"Who has independence?"

"White men."

It's a short conversation.

Do you feel independent?

With Love,
Greta

July 5, 1937

Dear Gertie,

I can lift my hand ever so slightly to pen to you that the

heaviness has returned. Heaviness is so easily forgotten when it's absent. My mind wants to collapse into nothing. But my body continues moving me about at the lowest possible energy. I am so close to a state of non-existence that I can see it.

With Love,
Greta

July 6, 1937

Dear Gertie,

Seeking death seems to be my routine after allowing myself the liberty of complex thought, then following it with spending considerable time with Bernard's family. Sitting with them at Lush Lake, celebrating this country's "independence," seems to result in my desire to shovel into the sand until I create a hole deep enough that makes everything around me—and everything in me—stop. Despite my desires, some strong force is keeping me moving on this earth. Though one might assume it's God, this force is far beyond my understanding of God.

With Love,
Greta

August 15, 1937

Dear Gertie,

I fear that I'll someday burst in laughter as I sit in church and listen to a man in a narrow white gown spew at a bunch of Poles with the hope that they see God in his Latin words. It's not that their innate ignorance is laughable; it's that I don't believe something as vast as the idea of God can be defined with words—Latin, or otherwise.

I don't believe it's necessary to force everyone to believe the words that are spit at them, or that we should erect ornate buildings around a belief. I don't think that financial gain or patriarchal power should result from sharing ideas.

Well, I got that off my chest. So at least that feels less heavy.

With Love,
Greta

August 28, 1937

Dear Gertie,

Do you think, as I do, that dialoguing about matters concerning the unseen should be free of any cost to those who participate?

With Love,
Greta

September 19, 1937

Dear Gertie,

I've learned enough Polish to understand that today Father Wójcik's homily was about how God designed women solely for bearing men's babies.

With Love,
Greta

November 4, 1937

Dear Gertie,

Many around here are upset because President Roosevelt said that the peace, freedom, and security of most of us in the world are being jeopardized by the ten percent who are threatening international order and law. I am thankful he had the courage to speak such sentiments, despite that so many American ears are closed off from actually hearing their meaning.

Do you think some people go through their entire lives with

fingers in their ears? Should wise men continue speaking to them anyway with the hope that a word of truth might someday slip past the barriers?

I feel less lonely since FDR spoke those words. I don't enjoy thinking that I'm the only one who can see beyond the present.

With Love,
Greta

December 7, 1937

Dear Gertie,

I find that the screams in my head increase during the holidays. It seems that there is even more work for me to do and more time to be spent with Bernard's family. Sometimes I wish I had the courage to let an audible scream erupt because it just might be forceful enough to carve a pathway to my freedom.

Do you think I seek freedom from my circumstances or from my mind?

With Love,
Greta

January 23, 1938

Dear Gertie,

I think religion in the wrong hands can be a weapon. Father Wójcik seems to enjoy preaching about the impropriety of Eve's descendants desiring to participate in activities that were made for men to enjoy. He is skilled at shooting holes into women.

With Love,
Greta

April 16, 1938

Dear Gertie,

Spring has arrived to my yard. I've been thanking the tulips and daffodils for choosing to emerge yet another time to add color to my world. I pray for that kind of resilience. I don't know how many springtimes I have left in me.

With Love,
Greta

October 9, 1938

Dear Gertie,

Helga pointed out a newspaper article about a doctor from New York who joined the Abraham Lincoln Brigade to fight in Spain's civil war. He isn't a white man and, no doubt, has endured his share of hardship in America.

Why is it so rare for an American man to have this kind of integrity that it becomes newsworthy?

Do you think suffering with prolonged hardship results in more thoughtful people?

With Love,
Greta

November 19, 1938

Dear Gertie,

The occurrence of Kristallnacht, and its aftermath requiring that Jews pay for their own destruction, proves to me that the light of this world grows increasingly dim. Perhaps it's always been dim, and my eyes are just now open enough to recognize that. What I see is that silence is suffocating the flame of morality.

Can you see light from where you are?

With Love,
Greta

December 4, 1938

Dear Gertie,

I have begun reading *The Evolution of Physics: The Growth of Ideas from Early Concepts to Relativity and Quanta*. It's by Albert Einstein and Leopold Infeld. Helga gave it to me. Someone left it behind at the Middleton Café and hasn't returned to claim it. I promised Helga I would give it back if someone returns for it because I know how valuable it is. It's signed by Albert Einstein, and I marvel that I'm able to hold the same book that he has held.

With this book I can learn about natural science. I'm still afraid to open the copy of the *Principia* Great-Grandma Anna gave me, which is unfortunate because I desperately want to know what's inside the book. I'm thrilled to have this physics book to read that doesn't have bloody handprints in it. But it does have Einstein's fingerprint! It appears that the ink dripped when he signed his name and he blotted it with his finger. Unfortunately, I have no one to discuss my discoveries with as I read the book. Helga is interested in political discussions but has no interest in physics. I will just discuss what I've learned with myself.

Being given this book may be the equivalent of having the Holy Grail placed in my hands because my analytical mind has already been awakened by its contents. There is a whole world of thought that exists independent from my knowledge of it.

Despite the information being new to me, this book makes my thoughts seem consequential. It's also a good reminder to me that evil men, and the havoc they wreak, are not the center of this universe.

I only read the book after Bernard goes to sleep. I carefully drape a blanket over the kerosene lamp and me so that Bernard doesn't catch me wasting time reading about such frivolous matters. I wish my body could be restored solely by reading instead of having to spend time sleeping each night.

I'm thankful that Einstein's book was abandoned in the café and landed in my hands. When I open it, it shines a ray of light into my darkness. Do you believe there is a God who intended for this book of non-religious truth to find its way to me?

> With Love,
> Greta

December 15, 1938

Dear Gertie,

It seems there is an entire world of discovery that has been kept from me. If I had been afforded time in schools of higher thought and a laboratory instead of in church and in the kitchen, who could I have become?

> With Love,
> Greta

December 18, 1938

Dear Gertie,

What if everything I've been taught about religion is wrong?

> With Love,
> Greta

December 30, 1938

Dear Gertie,

Do you know that two physicists from Germany have successfully split a uranium atom? It should be a good thing for science. But something is telling me that it is a bad thing for humanity.

Fritz Strassman and Otto Hahn are the physicists who split the atom. Do you think Ma's Hahn family and Otto's Hahn family come from the same people in Germany? If so, do you think opportunity—afforded or denied—might explain why people of the same ancestors evolve differently?

> With Love,
> Greta

January 15, 1939

Dear Gertie,

I'm puzzled over why this world's leaders are allowing the insane Adolf Hitler to run rampant. I don't understand why America doesn't open its doors wide and offer Jews escape from persecution when we have so much unused space here. The land in America existed before it was discovered. Shouldn't it belong to the world?

If I were president, I would invite the Jews in. Although, I know there is plenty of anti-Semitism they would have to face in this country.

Three of Bernard's brothers constantly spew vulgarities about the Jews and call them an "infestation."

> With Love,
> Greta

January 19, 1939

Dear Gertie,

Do you think consciousness is made of particles? If it is, where do those particles go when we die?

> With Love,
> Greta

January 29, 1939

Dear Gertie,

Jewish people continue to be plundered, raped, and murdered

in Europe. I find myself obsessing over when the moral world
will finally rise up and put a stop to the pogroms and evacuate the
concentration camps.

Where is Pope Pius XI's God? Why isn't God instructing
the Pope to rally to the defense of the Jews? Aren't the Jews God's
children too? Do all Catholic leaders share St. Augustine's belief that
Jews must suffer for eternity until they convert to Catholicism?

I think logic would be a kinder god for this world.

With Love,
Greta

February 11, 1939

Dear Gertie,

I read that, on his sixth anniversary as chancellor of Germany,
Hitler promised to exterminate the Jews if war against his country
occurs, and he ridiculed the Western Allies. He said it's shameful
that the democratic world is "oozing" sympathy, but doing nothing
to help. Hitler clearly is no idiot. Maybe he isn't insane. Perhaps he
is just another evil opportunist taking advantage of apathetic human
nature. Perhaps Americans who do nothing to interrupt Hitler's
schemes are just as evil as he is.

How do you define evil? Do you see any evil where you are?

With Love,
Greta

April 17, 1939

Dear Gertie,

I think hope is starting to return to this area. It looks as if
Bernard will be able to buy an automobile soon. If his mood
improves, I might ask if we can also purchase a radio.

With Love,
Greta

107

May 7, 1939

Dear Gertie,

I see more evidence of God in nature than I do in church.

With Love,
Greta

July 3, 1939

Dear Gertie,

I'm embarrassed to call myself an American. Along the eastern coast, there has been a refugee ship from Germany called the USS St. Louis with a thousand Jewish escapees from Nazi Germany on it. FDR ordered the Coast Guard to prevent any passengers from landing in this country. I believe he has just issued their death sentences by denying them safe harbor. Their future blood is on the hands of the United States.

What can I do to help when I have no power and only know of a God who continues to let such human atrocities happen? Do you know of a kinder god?

With Love,
Greta

July 4, 1939

Dear Gertie,

Do you think there is a place without politicians?

With Love,
Greta

September 8, 1939

Dear Gertie,

Bernard's family is quite distraught. Hitler invaded Poland

last week. He came in from the west. Warsaw was bombed and
Bernard's mother fears that her whole family there is dead. She
wishes she could go to Poland and help her people. I do too.
American leaders don't seem to care. I'm able to see the pattern and
where this will lead. Why can't they? At least other countries see the
logic behind declaring war on Germany to help Poland.

Germany's actions aren't helping my cause with Bernard's
family because they have found yet another reason to despise me for
my German ancestry.

With Love,
Greta

September 20, 1939

Dear Gertie,

Stalin also invaded Poland. It is now being attacked from both
sides, and America still doesn't seem to care. Bernard's mother is
treating me as if *I* am from the USSR, as well as being a German. She
is such an ignorant woman. I probably care about what happens in
Poland more than anyone she knows in America because I see what
is coming next. The world, as we know it, could explode.

With Love,
Greta

October 24, 1939

Dear Gertie,

This week I went to Orla Beach's wake in St. Paul. Cousin
Lucille gave me a ride in her Model A. I enjoyed seeing Martin again.
Though quite elderly, he continues to be a respectful man. It was
a pleasure to catch up with Walter and Mabel, who still reside on
Summit Avenue. Their son, Edward, didn't know who I was when
I said hello. But he remembered me once I said I was the girl who

went to see *Steamboat Willie* with him. He said he still catches himself counting on stairways because I made it so enjoyable for him. Though he has the same innocent face he had as a toddler, Edward has grown into quite a handsome young man, who is enrolled in high school. He strikes me as kind, like Walter and Martin. I'm pleased to see that he hasn't taken after his grandmother Orla. I enjoy seeing the proliferation of human decency.

After the funeral and luncheon, we went to a bar in St. Paul that Lucille was familiar with. We saw a few people marching on the sidewalks while carrying signs stating "No Foreign Entanglements." Lucille pointed at the signs and said, "Amen!" I refrained from opining because I had no other way of getting home.

I read in the newspaper that, according to a poll, 95% of Americans want to stay out of World War II. I guess I'm part of the 5% that believes those who are capable should lend a hand to others. I don't really support the concept of war; however, I believe that fascism in any country is bad for the whole world and should be stopped. Why can't others see we are each one tiny part of the greater whole?

I wish the world was free of political boundaries so that concerned citizens of the world could more easily right a wrong.

With Love,
Greta

November 3, 1939

Dear Gertie,

Bernard and I have been married eight years now and we still have no children. Rumors around Lush Lake have it that my womb is useless. I haven't said this to anyone, but I tend to believe the problem is in Bernard's parts because Aggie doesn't have any children yet either.

With Love,
Greta

March 9, 1940

Dear Gertie,

On our ride to church last Sunday, I begged Bernard not to buy a Ford because Henry Ford is an anti-Semite. Bernard called me a stupid woman who should mind my own business. After Mass, I solicited his father's advice on the matter. When we were all outside, I asked Johnny in Polish if he thought his son should be buying an automobile manufactured by Henry Ford. Johnny raised his eyebrows and said, "Ford is zło. That means evil." And then he spat on the ground.

Bernard bought a 1939 Chevy today.

With Love,
Greta

April 12, 1940

Dear Gertie,

Surely you must know how forlorn I am over the passing of Grandma Martha. Although I didn't see her frequently once she moved to Freedale, I found great comfort in knowing that she carried me in the warmest part of her heart every day of my life.

Who is left to carry me?

With Love,
Greta

May 13, 1940

Dear Gertie,

Germany has invaded the Netherlands, Belgium, and France. Do you think America should send help?

With Love,
Greta

June 4, 1940

Dear Gertie,

I was awakened this morning by the strangest dream about Grandma Martha giving me a radio. When she placed it in my hands, a jail door opened and released me.

With Love,
Greta

June 9, 1940

Dear Gertie,

A lawyer stopped by today to give me an inheritance check from Grandma Martha's estate. I'm going to go shopping for a radio and a map of the world.

With Love,
Greta

June 26, 1940

Dear Gertie,

According to radio reports, hundreds of Poles, including priests and teachers, have been sent to a concentration camp in Auschwitz. And France has capitulated to Germany. Why is no one stopping Hitler?

Do you think we are approaching the end of the world?

With Love,
Greta

August 7, 1940

Dear Gertie,

I wish I had more free time.

Today at the Middleton Café, I met Helga's cousin Friedrich.

He came to Minnesota from Germany five years ago. He was
holding a newspaper story about Auschwitz, so I asked him what
he thought about it. I noticed he struggled to find some of the right
words in English. So I spoke to him in Low German for a good
half hour about what is going on in Europe. We both enjoyed the
conversation. He invited me to meet at the café with a group of other
German speakers every other Thursday night. He said they enjoy
discussing current events, Nietzsche's views, and the meaning of life.
Although I sincerely thanked him for the invitation, I told him I did
not have enough time to spare for such enjoyable activities.

With Love,
Greta

September 17, 1940

Dear Gertie,

    Bernard is required to register with the local draft board next
month. Do you think I will shed a tear if Bernard's name is selected?

With Love,
Greta

October 9, 1940

Dear Gertie,

    There is a group called the America First Committee. They
want to keep the U.S. from intervening in Europe and are winning
the hearts and minds of Americans who struggle to think for
themselves. I wonder where such people originate; perhaps they
come from the darkest parts of Hitler's pockets.

With Love,
Greta

October 26, 1940

Dear Gertie,

I heard that Jews have been forced to build and pay for a wall around the Warsaw Ghetto. What kind of monster makes other people pay for a wall that he insists on creating? That's akin to handing someone a shovel and telling him to dig his own grave. I suppose it's the kind of monster the world creates with its apathy.

With Love,
Greta

November 6, 1940

Dear Gertie,

FDR was re-elected because he promised the country that no American boys would go to fight a foreign war. It seems he has perfected the art of telling the American people what they want to hear. I cast my vote his way even though I think he's wrong about not assisting in the effort to stop fascism. I cast my vote more enthusiastically for his running mate, Henry Wallace, because of his support for farmers and poor folks in the cities. Henry Wallace also supports scientific research in America. And he's more of a decent human being than most people I know.

With Love,
Greta

November 14, 1940

Dear Gertie,

I will put off sleep to write to you about something disturbing. I survived an event like no other that I have experienced.

Bernard had been intending to go duck hunting with his cousin Ambrose. But I sprained my ankle when I fell off a ladder the evening before and wasn't capable of caring for the cattle on my own.

Bernard cussed when it was decided that he had to stay home the next day.

He especially cussed me when a flock of ducks flew low over our house. Bernard grabbed his gun and shot a duck for dinner. He was outside in the warm weather butchering it when violent winds suddenly blew in. The sky darkened. I hobbled to the door and called to Bernard. He shouted that he would be in after finishing the chores. Shortly after that, the sky turned black. I limped to the basement to check the wood inventory for the furnace. Before I hurt my ankle, it had been my plan to haul wood in while Bernard was duck hunting. We had a day's worth under good conditions. It was clear that less than ideal conditions were descending on us. To conserve wood, I waited for Bernard to bring the duck in before starting the stove for supper.

Six o'clock came and went, and there was no sign of Bernard. I considered hobbling out to the barn to check on him. But I opened the door and found a foot of snow in front of me. The winds were blowing so hard that I couldn't see beyond a few inches in front of me.

I hoped that Bernard had the sense to stay in the barn. Bernard isn't known for his good sense, so I wasn't sure what the outcome would be. Around seven o'clock, I heard rapping at the bedroom window. I thought that the ghost girl from St. Owen might have finally found where I had moved to. When I went to see what was making the sound, I found Bernard standing outside the window, without a hat or jacket. He was nearly frozen.

I opened the window and asked why he was out there. He said he had been staying sheltered in the barn. When he thought the wind was dying down, he grabbed a lantern and attempted to run to the house. The winds picked up and blew out the lantern. Bernard lost sight of the house and eventually found himself in the gully by the road. He turned himself around and aimed for the house but kept walking in circles. He reached his hand out until he bumped into the ice house. After regaining his bearings, he aimed straight for the house and made contact at the bedroom window. He was so cold and so afraid to risk walking around to the door that I shoved the storm window out and helped him crawl into the house. It was quite the challenge to get him inside because his left hand was frozen to the partially butchered duck he was carrying. I quickly warmed a pail of water and submerged his hand and the duck until I was able to pry his fingers free. Then I peeled his wet clothes off and wrapped him in every blanket I could find in the house. I lit the kerosene lamp beside the wash tub in the cellar.

While Bernard waited in his bundle of blankets, I quickly poured what was left in the cistern into the tub. I melted pails of snow on the cookstove, carried them down the stairs, and poured them into the bath for him. I did my best to conceal the amount of pain I felt in my ankle as I carried the pails down the stairs because I knew he was in greater pain than I was. Bernard stepped into the tub and screamed when his toes hit the water. The temperature difference was too great for him. I went outside and got more snow to add to the bath to make it lukewarm. He crawled into it, and I gradually added warm water as he could tolerate it. I got his limbs thawed out and mixed warm brandy with honey to help thaw his insides and calm his nerves. Bernard expressed something close to appreciation for me that night.

And after his brothers stopped by to share some news this morning, Bernard expressed clear appreciation to me for hurting my ankle and causing him to stay home. They told him that yesterday Ambrose was found near the marsh he and Bernard always hunted in. He froze to death in the blizzard.

Do you suppose Bernard will appreciate me from this point forward?

With Love,
Greta

December 27, 1940

Dear Gertie,

I'm quite disturbed by a story that I heard about a Christian

Pole. He was killed in Warsaw by the Nazis for tossing a loaf of bread over the wall of the Jewish ghetto to help feed people on the other side.

Why aren't more of us tossing bread over ghetto walls?

With Love,
Greta

February 3, 1941

Dear Gertie,

Every time I feel bad about my lot in life, I think of a Pole or Jew in Europe suffering at the hands of Germans who would gladly trade his or her existence for mine.

Is it for divine reasons that I am here in America instead of suffering in Europe? Or is my existence simply a result of a lucky roll of the dice?

With Love,
Greta

June 29, 1941

Dear Gertie,

I heard Father Charles Coughlin on the radio, and wish I could scrub his voice from my mind. He praises Hitler for invading the USSR because he believes there should be a holy war on communism. He also condemns President Roosevelt for wanting to protect Jews from Germany and Italy. Father Coughlin is using the radio to speak poison into the minds of impressionable Americans. It angers me that he is posing as a servant of God to gain their trust and their devotion to his destructive words.

Do you suppose some people were born to annihilate others?

Is devastation built by nature into the rhythm of life? If so, do you think humans can transcend their natural limitations with morality?

> With Love,
> Greta

July 27, 1941

Dear Gertie,

FDR has frozen Japanese assets in our country. The pattern has continued unfolding around the world, and I believe this will have dire consequences for America. Should I call FDR on Johnny and Ludmila's telephone and let him know?

I wish I had a voice that mattered to powerful white men.

> With Love,
> Greta

August 2, 1941

Dear Gertie,

Do you think there could ever be one world without political boundaries?

> With Love,
> Greta

September 15, 1941

Dear Gertie,

Another hero of mine has fallen from the skies. Charles Lindbergh accused American Jews of "agitating for war." He said that Jewish influence is the greatest danger to our country. I think small-minded, self-oriented people like Charles Lindbergh are the greatest threat to America.

Do you suppose he was deprived of oxygen during one of his

long flights, or was he born without the bone of compassion?

With Love,
Greta

October 28, 1941

Dear Gertie,

The bluebird ghost girl appeared last night. She tapped me on the shoulder, and I asked her what she wanted. She laughed and said she wanted nothing. I stared at her as she held up one index finger. I opened my mouth to discuss the meaning of her action with her. But I swallowed the ghost and emerged from slumber coughing.

With Love,
Greta

November 29, 1941

Dear Gertie,

When will this madness stop? Fifty-two thousand Jews were murdered by the Nazis in Kiev, Ukraine. That is not an insignificant number of lives lost. America should not be withholding aid to Ukraine. Jewish children are being torn from their mothers' arms and are being put in cages by the Nazis. Although I don't have any children of my own, I still wonder what kind of monster one must be to put children in cages. If I ever have a child, I will count my blessings every day that I'm on American soil where a mother should never have to fear having a child torn from her arms.

FDR finally announced he would send aid to Soviets. People around here are not pleased.

With Love,
Greta

119

December 8, 1941

Dear Gertie,

Japan attacked Pearl Harbor yesterday. So here we are, engaged in war with Japan.

How does the war look from your perspective?

With Love,
Greta

December 11, 1941

Dear Gertie,

Germany and Italy declared war on the United States. Congress finally had the "courage" to declare war on their devastating impact on the world.

With Love,
Greta

December 15, 1941

Dear Gertie,

If there was a day set aside for everyone in the world to step into the shoes of the enemy standing next to him or her, do you think the origin of the enemy's position could be felt? Do you think we could then amend our treatment of one another and be at peace?

With Love,
Greta

January 3, 1942

Dear Gertie,

If there could be one world, I think it should not be ruled by one man but by a collective of human decency. Twenty-six countries have now agreed to work together to defeat the Axis Powers. I hope that will bring an end to the war.

With Love,
Greta

February 20, 1942

Dear Gertie,

President Roosevelt just signed Executive Order 9066. Why would he do that? I don't see how relocating Japanese Americans can result in anything good. Am I the only one who sees the illogical consequences of this order?

Maybe I imagined Order 9066 because this is America, isn't it?

With Love,
Greta

April 2, 1942

Dear Gertie,

Where am I?

Americans who have as little as 1/16 of Japanese ancestry have been imprisoned by the United States. I suspect that their only crime is being of the wrong heritage and skin color. How are the camps they are being relocated to any different than concentration camps? With Bernard's wire cutters, I want to run up to the gate of each internment camp and set the Japanese American prisoners free. If Bernard would allow it, I would invite every one of those falsely imprisoned Americans to live on our farm so they could have a safe haven in this "land of the free."

What is happening to our country? How do I know that I won't be forced to go to a German American internment camp for having 100% German ancestry? I have been exercising my first amendment right to speak freely against how we are engaging in war when I go to the Middleton Café. Do you think the FBI is monitoring me? It may be my good fortune that I don't have a telephone in my home.

With Love,
Greta

May 22, 1942

Dear Gertie,

Reason is far less powerful than a machine-gun in the hands of a madman. Thousands of Jews in Europe have been gunned down by the Nazis. When will these mass killings finally stop?

With Love,
Greta

July 18, 1942

Dear Gertie,

I find myself mournful today. I have become aware that progress in scientific discoveries has halted. The world's best scientific minds are needed for military matters. Science has become a weapon among competing powers.

With Love,
Greta

October 4, 1942

Dear Gertie,

Bernard has been in a good mood because there is a shortage of beer. He and his brothers have perfected the art of brewing and the Kozlowski brothers have become popular once again.

With Love,
Greta

November 19, 1942

Dear Gertie,

I wish I lived in a big city so that I could help build airplanes. I would enjoy putting my hands to anything that would soar in the future.

What would you be doing right now if you had a choice?

With Love,
Greta

December 20, 1942

Dear Gertie,

The Allies have finally publicly condemned the extermination of the Jews. Coverage of it on the radio and newspaper in America seems to convey less than half-hearted support for the condemnation. Where is the American outrage over lives lost? Pope Pius XII has been notably quiet on the matter. Where can morality be found? I don't trust that the Allies are engaged in this war for moral reasons, or they would have intervened long ago.

With Love,
Greta

February 15, 1943

Dear Gertie,

I've been even busier lately with the extra milking I have to help with. Johnny and Ludmila helped us buy two more cows so Bernard can continue qualifying for farm deferment from the war. Johnny and Ludmila are helping Bernard's brothers qualify for farm deferment too.

After church two weeks ago, I thanked Johnny for helping us buy the cows.

Johnny responded by swatting at the air and saying, "I am

selfish."

I was surprised by his statement, so I asked Johnny, "How is it that buying cows for us is selfish?"

Johnny reached in his pants pockets and showed me a roll of twenty dollar bills. "I saved my moonshine money for a rainy day." As he waved the bills, he said, "Rain is falling on the world, and I am selfish enough to buy my boys' freedom from the warfront."

I argued, "Those boys are helping to feed Americans. Rain is falling on the United States, too, because of the climate in Europe and Asia."

Johnny allowed himself a smile. He put his roll of bills back in his pocket, then put his hand on my shoulder and said, "You are a good girl, Greta."

Lately, I've been imagining what I would do if Johnny didn't have moonshine money to help Bernard avoid being drafted. I think I would like to enlist in the war so I can help stop fascism from raining on the world.

With Love,
Greta

February 17, 1943

Dear Gertie,

Helga at the Middleton Café is distraught. Her cousin Friedrich was sent to the internment camp at Fort Lincoln in North Dakota. He was accused of being part of a fifth column. Helga suspects that the only thing he was guilty of was discussing the meaning of life in Low German.

With Love,
Greta

March 4, 1943

Dear Gertie,

A group assembled in Madison Square Garden in New York to express their desire for the United States to support Jews in Europe. Do you think anyone cares about what they're saying—besides me?

With Love,
Greta

May 18, 1943

Dear Gertie,

Although I didn't think I could possibly be any busier, I am busier now that Johnny and Ludmila have purchased another milk cow and nine hogs for us. The farm deferment requirements increased again. I hope the requirement stops increasing because I'm not sure how much more responsibility I can take on. There is barely time to sleep—or write to you—as it is.

Though it took quite a bit of work to build a hog house and a pen, I have been enjoying the company of the hogs. They stink to high Heaven, but I think they are beautiful because they are so smart. All nine of the hogs seem to enjoy when I talk to them about mathematics, Albert Einstein's theories, and scientific discoveries. They are so smart that I'm thinking twice about ever eating bacon again. I'm thankful that Bernard refuses to eat pork and that these hogs won't end up on our table. But it will still be a difficult day for me when we send my smart friends to market.

With Love,
Greta

July 29, 1943

Dear Gertie,

Italy's fascist government has fallen! Mussolini was arrested.

125

There is one less person in this world with the power to persecute people. Should I bake a cake to celebrate?

With Love,
Greta

October 14, 1943

Dear Gertie,

I'm discovering that alliances among men are easily traded for something that serves them better. Italy has declared war on Germany.

With Love,
Greta

February 19, 1944

Dear Gertie,

Helga invited me to see *Casablanca* with her tonight at the theater in Gaston. She said she invited me to celebrate my birthday. But I know that I was actually invited because she is lonely again. Helga's second husband recently died when United States troops invaded the Marshall Islands.

With Love,
Greta

April 2, 1944

Dear Gertie,

The Chevy sits in the shed so much that I'm thinking of turning it into a brooder house. Gasoline is difficult to come by in this area.

With Love,
Greta

June 9, 1944

Dear Gertie,

I'm beginning to feel hope. Allied forces have invaded Normandy. I hope they are able to continue moving east until they scrub all Nazi sentiments from this world.

With Love,
Greta

July 18, 1944

Dear Gertie,

Though I would like to plump up and become more attractive, food beyond what we have on the farm is difficult to come by.

With Love,
Greta

August 10, 1944

Dear Gertie,

The IBM company has invented a machine called *Automatic Sequence Controlled Calculator*. It can do multiplication in six seconds, division in fifteen seconds, and a logarithm in under two minutes. I wonder if I can calculate as fast as this machine. Do you think all mathematics will be done by machines in the future? If machines take on the job of doing mathematics for everyone, what do you think people in the future will use their brains for?

With Love,
Greta

August 26, 1944

Dear Gertie,

Paris has been liberated from the Nazis! I believe the world is marching toward the end of this war.

With Love,
Greta

September 6, 1944

Dear Gertie,

I've been given yet another reason to dwell on the stupidity of powerful men who oppress other people. Last month, a man named Jackie Robinson was acquitted at his military trial in Texas. He was court-martialed for refusing to go to the back of a military bus when a racist bus driver told him to. Jackie Robinson was accused of behaving disrespectfully and failing to obey a command. I am thankful that Jackie Robinson was acquitted, and he won his battle with the military. But I am left to believe that the unnamed war being fought by non-whites in America will not be easily won.

With Love,
Greta

November 9, 1944

Dear Gertie,

What do you think of Harry Truman as FDR's new vice president? I voted for FDR but couldn't feel happy about my vote because of Truman. When he was in the Senate, he wanted to just let Germans and Russians destroy one another.

With Love,
Greta

January 12, 1945

Dear Gertie,

America finally decided last month to release the occupants of internment camps. The Supreme Court decided that, regardless of cultural descent, it isn't legal to detain loyal citizens without cause. Why wasn't that obvious to the men with power before people were interned? The only conclusion I can draw is that it *was* obvious. I suspect that many men with power are racists, with no appreciation for the value of any human life that is packaged differently than they are.

With Love,
Greta

March 24, 1945

Dear Gertie,

When I went out to the brooder house last week, I saw a strange balloon fly over the farm. It had something hanging beneath it. I ran to the barn to tell Bernard. By the time he got up from milking and came out into the yard with me, the balloon was gone. He looked at me with such contempt (I suspect for bothering him) and said to me, "*Wariat.*" That's Polish for *lunatic.*

Bernard says many derogatory things to me in Polish. I'm not sure whether he is aware of how much derogatory Polish I've learned since I've known his family.

I asked the neighbors if they saw the balloon. They didn't. There has been no mention of it in the newspapers. Maybe I am a wariat.

With Love,
Greta

April 13, 1945

Dear Gertie,

What do you think of Harry Truman as our president now

129

that FDR is dead? I'm not happy about it. I believe that something explosive is coming under his leadership.

With Love,
Greta

May 8, 1945

Dear Gertie,

I'm baking a cake to celebrate Hitler's suicide and the Axis Powers' surrender. I danced while I mixed it. Are you happy that the war with Hitler has ended? Do you think God will forgive me for celebrating suicide when it results in one less fascist in the world?

Now, if we could end the Pacific War without any more lives lost, perhaps this world could move forward.

With Love,
Greta

June 25, 1945

Dear Gertie,

What do you think about Ouija boards? I think they're ridiculous.

Bernard's sister Marcie brought one to Johnny and Ludmila's card party tonight. Shortly after I arrived, Aggie walked past me. I smelled her perfume, and I impulsively gagged. Marcie and Bernard's sister Stacia saw me gag and immediately started teasing that maybe I had morning sickness. To stop the conversation, I responded that a baby probably wasn't in my future.

Instead of stopping the conversation, Marcie went and got the Ouija board and told Stacia and me to join her in the back bedroom. I should have resisted, but I find myself always complying with Bernard's family to keep peace.

Marcie told me to pull up a chair beside the bed, so I did. She had Stacia join her on the bed. They sat facing each other with the board resting on their crossed legs. They each placed their fingertips on the edge of a triangular device called a planchette that had a glass window in it.

Marcie asked, "Spirits, are you there?"

The planchette glided over to YES.

Stacia asked, "Is Greta with child?"

The planchette slid over to NO even though it appeared that Marcie was trying to push it toward YES. I felt vindicated and should have walked out of the room at that moment, but I stayed. And the sisters continued with their game.

Stacia said, "It's probably a male spirit. They know nothing about buns in the oven." She looked at the ceiling and asked, "Are you a male?" The planchette immediately glided to NO.

After shooting Stacia a dirty look, Marcie looked up and asked, "Will Greta and Bernard have a baby?" The planchette circled around and around the board until finally resting at the edge, indicating no response.

The planchette was returned to the middle of the board and Stacia asked, "Will Greta and Bernard have a baby?" Again, the planchette circled around and around until it rested on the edge.

Angrily, Marcie shoved the planchette to the middle of the board and said, "God dammit, will Greta have a baby?!"

The planchette immediately pointed to YES.

Stacia giggled and said to Marcie, "The spirits are afraid of you, much like everyone else."

Marcie glared at Stacia, then she said, "Spirits, what can you tell us about the child?"

The planchette spun around the board and rested on the number one.

Marcie asked, "One child, one year from now, one what?"

Again, the planchette spun and rested on the number one.

The girls waited for the planchette to move. When it didn't, Stacia asked, "Will it be a girl or a boy?"

The planchette spun around and returned to the number one.

Marcie groaned and said, "Stupid spirits." She tossed the planchette across the room.

Stacia jumped up from the bed and said, "Let's play cards." And so I did.

With Love,
Greta

July 19, 1945

Dear Gertie,

What do you think of hatred?

I officially hate Bernard. I have had to put up with a lot concerning that man, and I don't care if he reads this—which he will probably try to do. When I came home from the women's church meeting this morning, I found him in his chair reading this book of my letters to you. He said I left it out on the bedroom dresser this morning, so he decided to read it. (I know that I would never leave it out, and I haven't written in it for weeks.)

Bernard told me I was insane for thinking he has had an affair with Aggie. I asked if he found her attractive because she is surely attracted to him. He said that she is pretty, and I never will be. He also said that doesn't prove anything happened between the two of them.

Bernard said to me, "Wariat!" And he tossed this book at my feet. I hate him. I have never felt so violated. These are my words—and your words. Why does he think he has a right to poke in my private life? He doesn't own me or my words. I hate him. I don't care what God thinks about my hatred. Why should I care about a God that doesn't care for me?

With Love,
Greta

P.S. I guess Bernard can read better than I thought he could.

July 31, 1945

Dear Gertie,

A bluebird landed on my kitchen windowsill this morning. The song it sang sounded as if it was composed just for me. The sweet sound lifted the sagging corners of my heart.

With Love,
Greta

August 2, 1945

Dear Gertie,

I ran into Raymond Redsun at the Tavern after visiting with Ma. He still makes the deepest part of me spring alive. I feel that he actually sees me when he looks at me with his eyes—which are the deepest brown I've ever seen.

I don't care if Bernard reads this. He deserves to. For every action there is an equal and opposite reaction. It isn't likely that he will read this though. When I'm not writing in it, I'm keeping this book of letters to you wrapped in a bread bag and buried at the bottom of the flour bin. Bernard has never baked in his life, and I'm sure he won't start now.

I also purchased a new diary to start writing in. I'll leave it in my dresser drawer so that Bernard can help himself to it. In it I plan to profess my love for Bernard. I will write that he is such a wonderful man, that I was a lunatic to ever think he would dally with another woman ... I will go on and on about how fortunate I am to have Bernard for a husband. I will denounce higher education, wise political moves, my views on economics ... I will give him every piece of bullshit that a man like him needs to feel big and in control of my life. And eventually, my private thoughts will actually become my own again.

With Love,
Greta

August 7, 1945

Dear Gertie,

Do you know that President Truman dropped an atomic bomb over Hiroshima in Japan? I don't think it was necessary. I do think it is a sad day to be an American.

With Love,
Greta

August 10, 1945

Dear Gertie,

I wept for the Japanese people in Nagasaki after we dropped the atomic bomb on them yesterday. America just doesn't seem to care about people in other countries.

With Love,
Greta

August 11, 1945

Dear Gertie,

I feel sick about dropping bombs on Japan. That kind of atomic energy should be used to accomplish something good. Bernard and his family are happy that the Japanese were bombed. Where are decent Americans?

With Love,
Greta

August 15, 1945,

Dear Gertie,

Do you think America is done with war since Japan surrendered? Do you think America has learned its lesson about the importance of helping to prevent war in the world? I fear that life is circular and that it repeats itself if there is no effort to change the natural course of a selfish human nature.

With Love,
Greta

September 5, 1945

Dear Gertie,

I was at Cousin Lucille's birthday party at the new Chance Hill Bar last night. Raymond Redsun was there too. Bernard didn't feel like going to the party because he had something to tend to "at the church." I knew he was intending to meet up with Aggie.

Ray walked over to me when he saw me in the bar. He pulled me away from the table and whispered in my ear. He said he was visited by Wakan Ozanzan. He asked me if I knew who that was. I told him I read about Wakan Ozanzan in a book I had been given when I was a child but didn't know anything beyond that one entry I read about him being hung at Fort Snelling. Ray then told me that Wakan Ozanzan gave him a message to deliver to the first beautiful woman he saw.

I was confused by what Ray was saying. But I asked what the message was to be polite.

Ray smiled and responded, "So you are aware that you are the first beautiful woman I have seen?"

I blushed and looked down at the floor. I noticed Ray was wearing work boots, and I wondered who he worked for or if he worked for himself. I suddenly wanted to know every detail about him. I looked into his eyes. I wondered if his eyes saw things differently than Bernard's eyes did.

Ray smiled at me again.

I willed myself to stop blushing—unsuccessfully.

He continued smiling with his eyes as he asked me, "Do you want the message?"

I couldn't help but smile back as I responded, "If a message from the ghost of Wakan Ozanzan is meant for me, I won't refuse it."

So Ray said, "The higher a bird flies, the smaller it appears to those on the ground."

Quite surprised by the message, I responded, "Nietzsche!"

Ray said, "Gesundheit."

I laughed and asked why he said that.

Ray smiled and said, "It sounded as if you sneezed, and I know that German is your mother tongue. Why did you make that sound?"

I answered, "It wasn't a sound. I was saying a name because I thought you were quoting Friedrich Nietzsche."

Ray shook his head and said, "No, I was repeating the words of Wakan Ozanzan."

Filled with confusion, I asked, "Why does Wakan Ozanzan want me to know that?"

After looking up for a moment, Ray said, "Perhaps he wants you to realize you are an eagle even if those on the ground mistakenly see you as something small."

Something that must feel like being truly cared for washed over me.

Ray must have noticed the change in my demeanor because he said, "Yes, he must care about you and your future. He must have seen it in the stars. Pass this wisdom on to others."

I couldn't stop smiling as I thanked Ray for delivering the message.

He smiled and thanked me for receiving it so graciously. Before he left, Ray said that he would be at the Chance Hill Bar every night next week after installing fencing on the dairy farm down the road. He said he hoped he would see me again soon.

Surprise filled my mouth, and I could find no words. So I just smiled and nodded. Ray smiled and nodded back at me. Then he headed for the door. As I headed back to the table where Lucille was sitting, I glanced over at the door. As Raymond crossed the threshold, I saw the ghost girl from St. Owen. She was holding an index finger in the air to make the number one. Do you think she knows Ray?

I have never met anyone like Raymond Redsun. He is real, isn't he?

With Love,
Greta

September 11, 1945

Dear Gertie,

I told Bernard that Ma is ailing, and I need to care for her for at least a week. Ma is still a tough old bird who can fend for herself, but I'm hoping to see Ray while I'm in Chance Hill.

With Love,
Greta

September 18, 1945

Dear Gertie,

Ray and I have gone on many walks by Raven Creek after dark. We go through the fields to get there so that we remain hidden and Chance Hill folks aren't given reasons to gossip. We also made visits to an abandoned house in the woods. Ray's father used to take him to the house when they went hunting together. He said it once belonged to a one-armed Irishman. It must have been the home of the Chance Hill peeper I heard about when I was young.

Ray enjoys being outside with me and talking about nature. He has a deep respect for the natural forces that govern everything. Ray says that everything that is truly known comes from the sun, air, water, and earth. He believes that we are not visitors on this earth, but we have sprung from this earth. He believes the earth is a part of every person—that we originate from the same elements—and we should treat the natural world around us with respect, as if it is our brother and sister.

I have discussed with him what I read about Einstein's discoveries in physics. Through conversation, it seems that his spiritual beliefs have similarities to new scientific understanding about the world. What if the Dakota are right to respect nature instead of believing in the white man's Messiah? What if understanding the ways of the earth is our real salvation? If it is, I hope I live long enough to see white men apologize for converting so many Dakota people to their religion.

With Love,
Greta

September 22, 1945

Dear Gertie,

I feel less alone when I can have meaningful conversation. I have never met anyone like Ray. He actually sees me when he looks at me. I truly hope he's real.

With Love,
Greta

October 3, 1945

Dear Gertie,

Bernard has been unusually kind to me lately. It must be because he has been reading my decoy diary. I know he has because I put three strands of hair in it that were gone each time I checked. I have filled the pages of the decoy with how wonderful Bernard is. As a result, he has been lying with me every night this week and can't seem to get enough of being inside me.

With Love,
Greta

October 11, 1945

Dear Gertie,

Bernard says he wants to buy me a book for Christmas. I had
written in my decoy diary that I love Bernard as much as books
and that I can't get enough of either one. Bernard says I should start
thinking about which book I want and to let him know by the end
of November so he has time to purchase it for me. At first, I was so
shocked that I said he didn't need to get me anything for Christmas.
But now I think I will ask him to buy me *Methods of Advanced
Calculus* by Philip Franklin.

With Love,
Greta

November 4, 1945

Dear Gertie,

Bernard took me dancing at the Chance Hill Bar last night. We
had such a grand time even though I was feeling a little off.

He enjoyed being with me so much that Bernard said he wants
to take me to a hotel in Mankato sometime. If he actually takes me
there, do you think Mankato is the farthest we will ever travel?

With Love,
Greta

November 30, 1945

Dear Gertie,

I think the United Nations seems like a good idea that will serve
this country well—as long as future leaders never adopt a nationalist
"America First" approach to international relations. The United
Nations should cause America to be more involved in international
crises.

I desire peace for everyone around the world. Do you think that is even possible? Whether or not it is possible, *I* will strive for peace.

Why do so few people seem to care about promoting peace? I don't understand why everyone can't see that accepting people as they are, instead of conquering their lands and their identities, would be in the best interest of the whole world. If the whole world could live in peace, I would name that place Just Be.

Why am I dwelling on such matters?

With Love,
Greta

December 3, 1945

Dear Gertie,

Although I have been so sick lately, I can't stop smiling. I'm with child—finally! I have suspected it for two months but wanted to be sure. The doctor just confirmed it, and I'm telling you first!

With Love,
Greta

December 13, 1945

Dear Gertie,

I keep thinking about how, in just six months' time, I will have completed my contribution to creating a human being. The notion could almost make me feel like a Creator. But I think that this creature growing inside me will somehow make *me* complete after nine months.

This child will understand the importance of promoting peace. I will do everything in my power to make sure that happens. And I hope my child will teach his or her child the importance of promoting peace, and so on. If every parent expecting a child right now handed newborns the torch of peace, how long do you think it would take to achieve peace across the world?

With Love,
Greta

December 26, 1945

Dear Gertie,

Ray has left for a spiritual journey. I saw him this morning at the Engel Christmas party at the Chance Hill Bar. Sadness hung from his shoulders as he briefly spoke to me by the back door. He said he has lost his guardian spirit. He needs to find it and consult with it because he has a decision to make. Ray didn't tell me what he needs to decide on. I want to run and catch up to him. I want to spend every day with him so he can look at me and tell me that I am seen, that this life inside me is real.

I have no idea if Ray will ever return to me.

With Love,
Greta

January 10, 1946

Dear Gertie,

I must stop letting my mind trail after Ray so I can turn my thoughts to properly preparing for my child. Something in me is telling me to stop thinking about running. I've decided to stay put and make the most out of the reality that surrounds me.

With Love,
Greta

March 3, 1946

Dear Gertie,

An electrical power line will make its way to our home next

month. Our neighbors are all abuzz with talk of soon being able to purchase milking machines, poultry lights, electric lanterns, electric ranges that don't require wood, refrigerators that don't require ice blocks, clothes washers that don't require the use of my hands, irons that don't have to be heated on the stove ... What a gift electricity will be to my life! What will I do with all my excess time in the future?

Do you think I might have time to read each day?

With Love,
Greta

April 2, 1946

Dear Gertie,

I read that the last Japanese American internment camp has been closed. I hope that is the last of internment camps ever to be constructed in this country. And I hope it is the last time innocent people have to experience incarceration in America.

With Love,
Greta

June 3, 1946

Dear Gertie,

Bernard's family threw me a baby shower. I received plenty of blankets and bibs with *Dziecko Kozlowski* embroidered on them. I guess they have decided this will be a Polish baby.

With Love,
Greta

June 11, 1946

Dear Gertie,

I've been thinking about the ghost girl who told me to subtract the sum from the chosen number. Though I haven't deciphered the meaning, I will continue dwelling on it until I do.

Perhaps I have too much time on my hands if I'm indulging in thinking so frequently.

The doctor told me I will have to spend two weeks in bed after the baby is born. Although I found that to be foolish at first, I have decided to ask Cousin Lucille to help care for the baby during that time so I can finally finish reading Ellen Egan's book that Great-Grandma Anna gave to me. I've been wanting to finish reading the last half of it ever since I was a child so that I could take the entire walk through Ellen's journey. I wondered what happened after the hanging at Fort Snelling and often desired to read the rest of the book after I was married. But I didn't want Bernard to catch me spending time on it. I worried that if he caught me with the book, he would tear it from my hands and toss it into the fire.

What do you think should happen to Ellen's book when I pass away? I think her words are deserving of a special place in this world.

With Love,
Greta

June 25, 1946

Dear Gertie,

My sweet Sally was born this morning. She has dark hair. Her eyes are the deepest brown I've seen. And I believe that she already sees me when she looks at me. I am here. She is here. She is mine to hold. And I think she is the most beautiful creature.

I hesitate to let Ma hold Sally whenever she decides to come meet her granddaughter. I fear that her way of being is contagious. Although I know it probably isn't, I would prefer that Sally not see that such despicable things exist in this world. I want Sally to believe that a peaceful existence is possible.

I may have to say good-bye to you, Gertie, as I put my diary away for a while. Even though I still love you as much as I did in the beginning, I want to give my daughter every spare minute of my time that I possibly can. I intend to love Sally more than any mother has loved a child and give her the message that this country belongs to her. I want her to know that she lives in a place where any dream can become a reality.

With Love,
Greta

P.S. I still desire to travel faster than the speed of light to be with you. But I no longer wish to be a two-dimensional character in a story where we meet again. I have discovered that being three-dimensional in a four-dimensional setting with electricity running through it isn't so bad. I have also realized that the most desirable path to take from one point in life to another is not a straight line. Spacetime dictates the way in this world; the beauty of the journey through it makes every destination worth the wait.

WHEN LIFE WAS STILL

Book Three: Amy

Julie A. Ryan

SO LOVELY WAS THE LONELINESS OF
THE LAND O' LAKES!

This belongs to:
Amy Clausen

(But really, it belongs to Ms. Pratt at Middleton High School. I can't call it mine when she's telling me what I have to write about for Practical Comp. assignments. So if I lose this notebook and you find it, give it to her.)

9/6/1983

Ms. Pratt, no offense, but don't you think "Practical Composition" is a bit of an oxymoron? I can think of more practical things to do with time than composing essays about my life—like watching MTV.

~ Amy

<u>My Favorite Place</u>

The peanut shells on the floor of the Chance Hill Bar, tossed there by thirsty men, sit on top of other remnants of my childhood. Under my favorite table near the dance floor, I pressed my palms into the up-turned shells and traced the interesting figure eight shape they left on my four-year-old hands. When I was a little older, Joey told me I was stupid for thinking it was a figure eight when it was actually called "infinity." As my brother, who is three years older than me, he has made it his job to teach me things like that and to tell me how stupid I am.

After he told me about infinity, I frequently thought about it as I drew it on my palm. Joey told me that infinity meant no beginning and no end. That it always was and always will be, like God. He was always saying things like that and talking about God a lot when we were little even though he's a total druggie with a mohawk hairdo now. When he talked that way, I noticed it made the old women we knew from Chance Hill very happy. They would say, "Oh, Joey, you're such a smarty. Such a good boy." Nobody bothered to say anything to me because I didn't talk about infinity, or God, or anything at all, really. I simply sat under tables and watched people say nice things to Joey. Maybe people talked to him more because he has blonde hair and blue eyes, and my hair and eyes are very dark brown.

On Saturday nights Joey would dance with all the old women at the Chance Hill Bar, even the ones he didn't know. Nobody sat at the end table by the dance floor on the weekends because they didn't want to risk getting kicked by people doing the polka while the Novak Brothers Junior band played. I loved having the floor under the table to myself. I've always been small compared to everyone else my age. But I've always liked that I could go where other people can't. I think I'm the only person who was aware of what was under the heels of the women of Chance Hill. They bared their soles to me like clockwork as they swung past my table that sat in the two o'clock position of the dance floor. All the women followed the lead of the men moving to the rhythm of the oom-pah band. But, with the way the women kicked their feet like rudders, it flashed an omen to me that they would eventually be revealed as the true driving force of the world.

Every Saturday I tried to push my hands into the peanuts so hard that the shells would become part of me. It was my dream to be Amy the Human Peanut so I could travel with the carnival that came to Gaston County every year. Once, when Grandma Greta Kozlowski took Joey and me, she paid twenty-five cents each so we could walk through a converted trailer home to see a boy who had fish scales all over his body and watch a guy shove nails up his nose and spit them out his mouth. Amy the Human Peanut would have fit in well with them.

When I took a break from creating peanut skin, I enjoyed watching Grandma Greta leaning on the bar. It's one place I could see her relax. I always knew I would find her standing beside Grandpa Bernie, who always sat on the bar stool closest to the men's room. Grandpa and Grandma are the ones who took Joey and me to Chance Hill every Saturday night. We lived with them while my mom, Sally, and dad, Benny, were in Africa. My parents got married just six weeks after they met at a drive-in movie toward the end of their senior year of high school. They both joined the Peace Corps instead of going to college.

Most people don't know that I'm African because I was born in Ghana. I was actually born the day Bobby Kennedy died on June 6, 1968. I sometimes wonder if his soul slipped into my body when he passed because I totally get what he was all about. I was born in Ghana because Mom and Dad found a way to stay there and help people after their volunteer commitment to the Peace Corp was done. Mom brought me to Minnesota when I was a baby. After being in America for a few months in 1968, Mom felt really sad about the political climate. She had a tough time listening to George Wallace. When she saw a re-run of candidate Richard Nixon saying, "Sock it to me?" on *Laugh-In*, she had reached her American politics saturation point and decided to return to Ghana to be with my dad, who was teaching Africans how to grow food. Mom thought that was a place where she could contribute to a less frivolous society in a meaningful way. Mom left me with Grandpa, Grandma, and Joey to be raised in a frivolous society. My mom is Grandma and Grandpa's only child. I've noticed they do whatever she tells them to, like raise her kids for her—even though it resulted in plenty of exposure to Richard Nixon in our formative years. Grandpa Bernie LOVED Nixon. Grandma Greta loved Hubert Humphrey. I'm a lot like Grandma Greta. Sometimes I find it hard to believe that I'm even related to Grandpa Bernie. He's made of different stuff than I am.

I was fine with being raised by my grandparents when I was little. Grandma Greta never yelled at me or Joey, even when we deserved to be yelled at. We should have gotten yelled at when Joey and I emptied the old basement refrigerator while she was in the garden. It was Joey's idea. Stuff like that was always Joey's idea. I did everything he told me to do, and I'm not sure why. He said he needed to know if the light goes off when the refrigerator door is shut. Joey said I needed to get inside so he could find out the answer. So after we emptied the refrigerator and took out the shelves, I climbed in. Joey shut the door, I told him the light was off, but he didn't respond. I yelled to him that the light was off and still heard no response. When I pushed on the door, it wouldn't open. I've never liked the dark, so I screamed for Joey to let me out. My screams turned into crying. I wet my pants because I was so scared. And then I cried even harder when I realized that Grandma Greta would probably have to throw out the refrigerator because I had peed in it. The hardest part was waiting for someone to notice me. I fell asleep crying and didn't wake up until Grandma opened the refrigerator door when she went down to get extra eggs for the lemon meringue pie she was making for supper. Instead of yelling at me for peeing in her fridge, she scooped me up, wrapped me in her favorite patchwork quilt, and held me in her arms until I warmed up.

I knew Grandma and Grandpa loved me. And I loved our Saturday night routine when I was young. At the Chance Hill Bar, I would get to see Grandma smile really big. That bar was, and still is, the only place where she appeared to like Grandpa Bernie at least a little bit. She liked that place so much when I was little that we were always the last to leave on Saturday night. Even though we had to be up early the next morning to get the cows milked before heading to church, we stayed to help clean up the bar. I'd help by drinking the leftover beer from people's glasses. It was before I cared about germs and things like that. It took me a while to realize that the nauseated feeling I had on Sunday mornings wasn't necessarily caused by attending Mass. It was probably from all the beer and backwash I drank the night before.

Who is Gertie?

Find out in the next book

of the WHEN LIFE WAS STILL trilogy

Book Three: Amy

For updates on sequels and spin-offs, please visit:

www.WhenLifeWasStill.com

Something Predictably Beautiful

from

WHEN LIFE WAS STILL

· B O O K   O N E ·

"Choose a number greater than twenty."
"Add the digits of your chosen number."

· B O O K   T W O ·

"Subtract the sum from the chosen number."

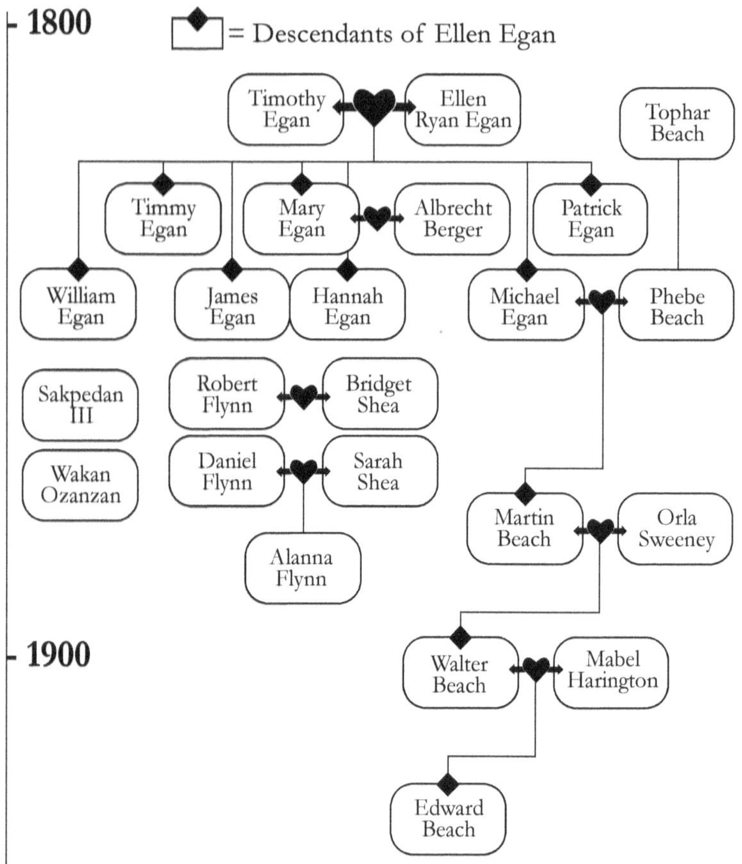
= Descendants of Ellen Egan
1800
Timothy Egan
Ellen Ryan Egan
Tophar Beach
Timmy Egan
Mary Egan
Albrecht Berger
Patrick Egan
William Egan
James Egan
Hannah Egan
Michael Egan
Phebe Beach
Sakpedan III
Robert Flynn
Bridget Shea
Wakan Ozanzan
Daniel Flynn
Sarah Shea
Martin Beach
Orla Sweeney
Alanna Flynn
1900
Walter Beach
Mabel Harington
Edward Beach
2000

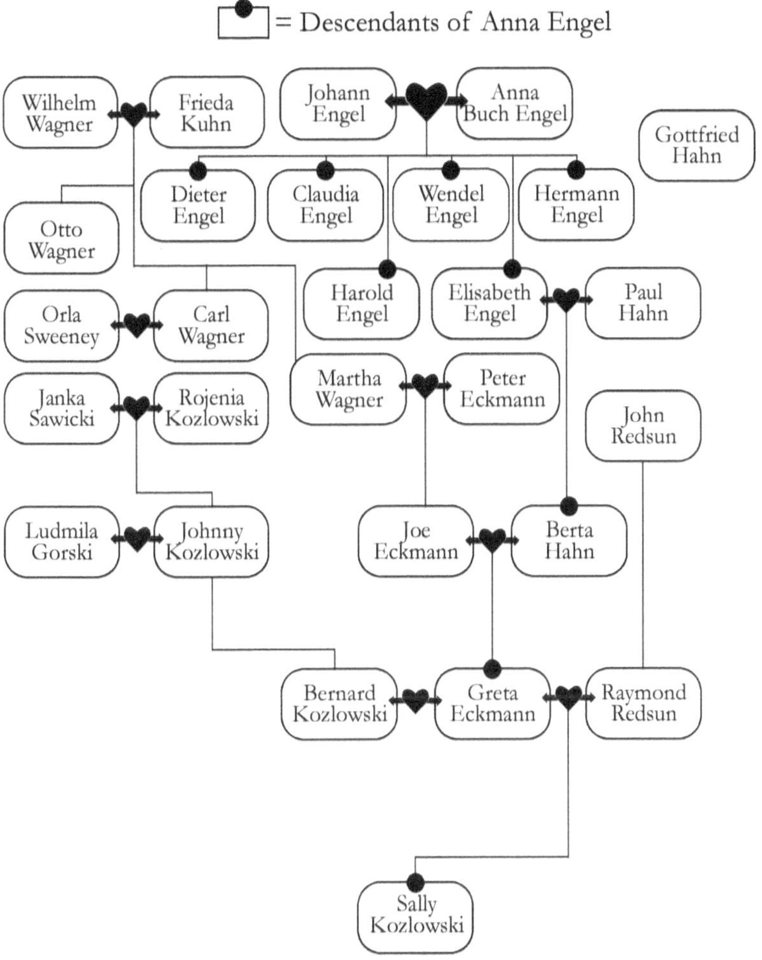

The Families of WHEN LIFE WAS STILL
Book One and Book Two

= Intimate Relationship

Acknowledgements

I am grateful to everyone who has refused to accept the stillness of inequality and has resisted abuse of power. This world continues to move because of you.

Thank you, Team Hillary, for running and putting that reverberating crack in the glass ceiling that sits on American women. You won in my book.

Thank you, Amy Klobuchar, for getting to work and getting the job done. You're an inspiration for Minnesotans and a beacon of hope for America.

Thank you, my immigrant ancestors, for finding your way to America.

Thank you, Andrew, for draping genealogical flesh on Ellen's missing bones and giving me the impetus to create a new world for her to explore.

Thank you, Luv Burns, for haunting my childhood home and for continuing to be my muse.

Thank you, my fellow writers, for providing regular feedback and encouragement over the past five years. You've been a wonderful captive audience.

Thank you, Mom and Dad, for giving me a fascinating history and sharing stories that have influenced my writing. I deeply appreciate that you granted me the freedom to be me during my fun rural Minnesota upbringing. Through your example, I knew that the "me" I wanted to be was one who practiced human decency.

Thank you, Vinny, for patiently letting me bounce ideas off you for this trilogy. Your respectful insight, your unbelievably supportive nature, and your faith that I would do something meaningful with my storytelling ability coaxed me out of the quicksand of discouragement countless times. Thank you for encouraging me to fly and for taping my wings back on every time they fell off.

Thank you, Keegan, for your mathematical expertise. From the beginning you've shown me new angles from your perspective. Thank you for teaching me how to properly pursue all my dreams by demonstrating how to get from here to there.

Thank you, Lyn, for your desire to make a stand against social injustice. Your opposition to complacency and resulting passion for reform is truly inspiring.

Thank you, Evan, for thinking that I'm somebody special, for laughing at my jokes, and for making me want to be good at something other than badminton and croquet.

Thank you, Barb, Gina, Colin, and Vince, for your willingness to read (and re-read) my manuscript, your editorial input, and your constructive feedback. The reflections you shared added significant depth to my words. This version of the story exists because of you.

Thank you, Haley, for generously sharing your amazing creativity with me. Everything you touch with your imagination becomes more beautiful. My dream of publishing this trilogy wouldn't have made its way to the world without your willingness to help make it come true. Life is a better place because of you!

About the Author

Julie Ryan is a novelist, essayist, poet, and artist who views everything through a satirical lens. She has always been interested in humanitarian issues. Even as a child, she felt it was her duty as a human being to speak out against social injustice—way before it was cool. Her sense of humor and obsession with justice for all seeps into each of her creations. In this era of political blunders that begs for comic relief, she feels it's time for this trilogy.

www.WhenLifeWasStill.com